Praise for *the watcher*:

"These three remain strangers who barely speak to one another, but Howe draws them together in haunting, magical ways. Each has the vivid sensation of floating or flying; each is truly confused about whether some event was imagined, or dreamed, or had actually happened; each is afraid to want something too badly. Their deep-down link, pulling all of them under, is loss—devastating loss that reveals itself slowly, with ever-growing intensity for the reader."

—*New York Times Book Review*

"Hypnotic . . . a powerful novel."—*Toronto Star*

"Lyrical and literary, Howe's experimental novel is a challenging and wholly original story."

—*Detroit Free Press*

"*the watcher* is a novel so powerful that even after the last page is read . . . [Margaret's] story may be reflected upon again and again."

—*School Library Journal*

An ALA Best Book

the watcher

JAMES HOWE

aladdin paperbacks
New York London Toronto Sydney Singapore

In addition to thanking Betsy Imershein, I wish to express my gratitude to my editor, Jonathan Lanman, for his insight, clarity, and unwavering faith in this book and its author. My appreciation goes as well to Dr. Kenneth Meyer and Dr. Sharon Farber for their generous support and wise counsel, and to Alison Marra.

First Aladdin Paperbacks edition June 1999
Second Aladdin Paperbacks edition March 2001
Copyright © 1997 by James Howe

"YOU CAN'T ALWAYS GET WHAT YOU WANT"
Written by Mick Jagger & Keith Richards
© 1969 ABKCO Music, Inc.
All rights reserved. Reprinted by permission.

Aladdin Paperbacks
An imprint of Simon & Schuster
Children's Publishing Division
1230 Avenue of the Americas
New York, NY 10020

Also available in an Atheneum Books for Young Readers hardcover edition.
Designed by Ann Bobco and Patti Ratchford.
The text for this book was set in Bembo.
Printed and bound in the United States of America
10 9 8 7 6 5 4 3 2

The Library of Congress has cataloged the hardcover edition as follows:
Howe, James, date.
The watcher / James Howe.—1st ed.
p.   cm.
Summary: As she sits watching a seemingly perfect family and a handsome lifeguard on the beach, a lonely, troubled girl projects herself into the fantasy lives she has created for them.
ISBN: 0-689-80186-6 (hc.)
[1. Family problems—Fiction. 2. Child abuse—Fiction. 3. Beaches—Fiction.]
I. Title.
PZ7.H83727Wat   1997
[Fic]—dc20
96-43045
ISBN: 0-689-83533-7 (Aladdin pbk.)

To Betsy

the watcher

You can't always get what you want

But if you try sometimes,
You just might find

You get what you need.

—*The Rolling Stones*

•

The girl had no memory
no real memory
The girl had no real memory of how she came
to this place. It was a dream

Except for the dream which was so real it felt
like a memory

The dream of having a family once and losing
them.

The girl had no real memory of how she came to
this place, except for the dream which felt so real it
might have been a memory. The dream of having a
family once and losing them. Had there been a
shipwreck? Is that how she and her family came to be
came to be washed ashore and separated?

What did it matter if it was real or a dream?
The fact is that the girl had lived all her life all the
life she could remember
on this island where no one lived
where no one else lived that she knew of,
except for the beast who kept her captive
and the and the doll?
and the enchanted doll.

a house full of strangers

The bitter taste of lead brought her to her senses. How long had she been sitting there, lost in thought? She lowered the pencil, tucked it into the small notebook on her lap, and in its place drew in an oily strand of hair, which she sucked and nibbled like a hungry little mouse.

It was the first day. Miraculously, they had allowed her to go out by herself, and she had almost at once found this safe place, this spot at the top of the stairs where she could sit and watch the others on the beach. It was early yet, and a weekday, so the beach was nearly empty.

She was glad for that. It made it easier to believe she was invisible when there were fewer eyes to see her. What would they have seen, anyway? A bony girl with loose brown hair falling across her face and shoulders. A baggy T-shirt and pink and powder-blue flip-flops, one of which was held together with packing tape. That's all. Just her body, just her clothes. They would not have seen *her*. No.

Her parents had never rented a house at the beach before. The fact that they had done so for an entire month filled her with feelings so unfamiliar she had no names for them. Still, it was good to be filled with *something,* even feelings without names. It was, she imagined, a little like having a birthday party—something she had never actually had—and all the guests being strangers. A house full of strangers, but a full house.

It did not occur to her to sit on the beach. She hadn't brought a towel to sit on, for one thing. She wasn't even wearing a bathing suit under her T-shirt, just shorts. It didn't matter. She was content to be where she was, slightly above, at a little distance from the people and the sand and the sea that stretched out forever. From where she sat she could watch the children on their pudgy legs run to the water's edge and fill their buckets, then scamper back to the safety of their mothers, shrieking and laughing as the waves rolled up behind them, nipping at their heels: tag, you're it. She could almost smell the lotion the mothers squeezed out of tubes into the palms of their hands and rubbed lovingly over their little sons' and daughters' browning bellies and fiery backs. She could watch umbrellas pop open like bright flowers bursting into bloom, and these made her think of the clusters of crocuses that appeared in her backyard each spring, always catching her by surprise, bringing with them as they did the memory of hope.

But what she watched most intently were the families—not *pieces* of families with only a mother or a nanny, but what she thought of as *complete* families with two parents and at least two children, preferably a girl and a boy.

There was only one such family on the beach that morning, and she found it not only complete but nearly perfect. It was the little girl who had caught her eye, but it was the girl's brother who held it. He appeared to be about thirteen, her age, although he might have been a little older. He was a good deal older than his sister, that much was clear. He had a long, thin body, the kind she had once read described as "lanky." It wasn't his body that interested her, though, but his manner—the way, for instance, he dug a long trough in the sand for his sister to sit in, then knelt before her, listening patiently to all her instructions before beginning the elaborate sand fin that would turn her into a mermaid. It seemed, as far as she could tell from where she sat, that the boy had real artistic talent. She wondered if his father was an artist, because she noticed that he sat sketching his children as they played together.

She expected the boy to run off at some point, to join friends and leave his sister behind. But he never did. He seemed to enjoy being with her, and when he took her hand at one point, it was such a natural gesture that she felt certain he'd done it many times before. And when, later in the day, after she had been watching the family for a long time, she saw the boy bend down and kiss, actually kiss, the top of his sister's head, she became so dizzy she was forced to drop her head to her knees and think of other things until the dizziness went away.

She turned her attention to the others on the beach. It was getting late. People were packing up and leaving. The only new arrivals were some boys carrying surfboards. She cringed when they charged down the steps past her; she found their buzz-saw voices and masculine posturing repulsive.

It was then that she realized how much she'd been watching someone else that day, someone other than the family. Mostly she had watched the back of his shoulders and neck and head, all golden and bronze, because that was all she could see when he was sitting, which he was most of the day. But from time to time he had stood up, to blow his whistle or wave his arms or stretch. And on occasion he had jumped down to run into the water and pull out a floundering swimmer or go for a swim himself; those were the times she liked watching him most.

When he walked past her to leave or return to the beach, he did not speak to her or acknowledge her in any way. Which of course made sense because he could not see her. She was invisible.

But she saw *him,* and though she did not understand it—how different could he be, after all, from those rowdy boys with their surfboards; a little older, perhaps, but cut from the same mold—she thought him beautiful. More beautiful than anyone she had ever seen.

If it had happened somewhere else, she might have found this unlikely response of hers more disturbing than exciting, but here—in this magical place that was so like the crocuses in spring—it was just the opposite. Here, she thought, here she could live in a house full of strangers and feel at home.

•

How could the girl have known there was an angel?

She had always been a prisoner. She had seen nothing of the island but what the beast had allowed her to see.

Then one day while the enchanted doll sang her sad song a key fell from her pocket. The girl quickly grabbed it up before the doll could notice.

For when the doll was under the spell of the music she saw and heard nothing. And so the girl was able to unlock the door and slip away. The beast was sleeping in the shade of a tree. He was in a stupor. All around him were the bones of his last meal. The girl shivered. The beast ate animals without killing them first.

Scarcely daring to breathe, the girl tiptoed past the beast until she reached the gate and was free.

In the distance, she could hear the steady roar of the ocean. She ran along strange paths, past wild blueberry bushes and tall reeds whispering reeds

wild blueberries and whispering reeds

until she came to the dunes and then she ran across those and at last she came to the ocean.

Her heart was happy and sad at the same time.

Happy because the ocean went on forever and promised freedom.

Sad because the ocean surrounded her little island and meant prison.

The girl began to cry.

Then she heard the fluttering of wings.

And there,

There, standing atop a wooden tower at the ocean's edge, she beheld an angel folding his cloud-white wings close against his golden body.

He was gazing out at the ocean, his head held high and proud. He did not see the girl.

Where had he come from? Why was he there?

Perhaps the girl had prayed without knowing, and the angel was the answer to her prayer.

he could
see himself floating

Chris Powell was distracted. His partner had asked him twice if he wanted a stick of gum, and both times he'd said no without knowing what he'd been asked. It wasn't like Chris to be distracted; he wasn't what you'd call a thinker. The whole business was making him downright uncomfortable, if you want to know the truth.

"You feeling all right?" Jenny asked.

"No," Chris said, without looking at her. "Yeah, I'm okay."

It wasn't that Chris didn't feel like talking to Jenny, he just didn't feel like talking. Something was trying to work its way up inside his brain to where he could grab hold of it, and until it got there he had to keep the pathways clear. The problem was, he didn't have much experience with this sort of thing. With all these thoughts drifting in and out of his head like so much flot-sam and jetsam, how was he supposed to know which was the one distracting him?

"Chris, wake up!" Jenny snapped. "Didn't you hear me say I'm going in? I got a kid in trouble here. Come on, get with the program!"

He watched Jenny run down the beach to pull a winded toddler out of the surf. From the look of it, the kid had been caught in a back-wash. Where the hell were the parents, anyway? He imagined the mother looking up from some trashy paperback she was probably reading and running to wrap herself around her bawling kid. *My poor baby, are you all right? Mommy's here now, don't cry, don't cry . . .*

Don't cry, shit. Lucky for you, lady . . .

Chris reminded himself to turn his atten-tion back to the ocean. Why was he having so much trouble keeping his mind on the job today? Hey, it wasn't just today. Lately, there had been times he found himself getting lost out there, when he could see himself, honest-to-God see himself, floating in the air out there, hovering over the ocean like one of those blimps advertising sunblock or some crazy thing. No, more like a pelican on the lookout for a tasty fish, gliding, drifting, riding the wind until it swooped down and nabbed that sucker up in its beak. Only, Chris didn't swoop. He just floated, drifted, looking, not knowing what he was looking for.

And all the time that he was out there floating he never moved from his seat atop the lifeguard stand, elbows propped on knees, the cord of his whistle always in motion, twirling clockwise around the index finger of his left hand, then counterclockwise, then clockwise. Tick. Tock.

Jenny climbed back up the stand, the smell of the surf clinging to her wet skin.

"Nice save," Chris said evenly.

"Tweren't nothin'," chirped Jenny, which Chris knew basically to be true. Lifeguards made this kind of save every day. As far as he was concerned, you could hardly even call it a save when all you did was pull somebody out of water you could stand in. Even in deeper water, a rescue wasn't usually a matter of life and death, although he knew—because he'd heard it about a million times in training—any trouble in any water had the potential of being life or death.

Still, he'd never saved anybody from drowning—not the *real* life-or-death thing, anyway. Sometimes, when he was hanging out with the other guards, Chris would let on that he couldn't wait for the chance to be a big hero. But the truth was—and nobody knew this, *nobody*—he was scared he'd blow it and instead of being a hero . . .

The movement of Jenny's arm as she slicked her lips with gloss caught Chris's eye. He moved his head a few degrees past her to see if he could get a glimpse of the girl on the steps.

He didn't know how he knew she was watching only *him* and not *them*. He could just feel it. Every day, usually an hour or so after he came on duty, he'd sense that she was there. He never saw her arrive. He'd just turn his head and there she'd be: sitting on the same top step, leaning her shoulder against the same two-by-four upright, holding him with her gaze as if it were a microscope and he a measly amoeba.

She was, what, twelve maybe. At first, Chris had been sure she was just another lifeguard groupie. They came with the job, and Chris wouldn't say he minded, even if most of them weren't ripe for the picking, so to speak, so the most you'd better play with were your eyes and keep your hands to yourself. But there were a couple of things wrong with this one. She never came over to the stand, for one thing, never approached him or said *hi* if he happened to pass within twenty feet. She never smiled. And she was always alone.

And, always, it seemed to Chris, watching him.

It was a few days after he'd first noticed her that he'd started feeling distracted. It was like being with somebody who drops some tiny object on the ground, a contact lens or an earring, and you spend an hour trying to help them find it, and pretty soon it becomes an obsession, you *have* to find it, you keep looking, maybe the person who lost it isn't even there anymore, maybe you've even forgotten what it is you're looking for, but you keep looking because you have to, because suddenly your whole life is about looking, and you realize that you've never really looked for anything before, not really.

Chris shook his head, half expecting it to rattle, wondering what the hell was making him think this kind of shit.

"Look," he heard Jenny say.

He turned to his left. A girl (seven? eight? Chris had this need to guess kids' ages. He wasn't all that good at it, wasn't even all that interested, just needed to do it for some reason) was being turned into a sand mermaid by an older boy (fourteen? fifteen?).

"I like how he did the scales," Jenny said.

Chris lifted his mirrored sunglasses and squinted to get a better view. Grunting, he lowered the glasses as the boy said something and the girl laughed. He watched the boy run to fetch the parents, who put down their books and came to see. They patted the boy on the shoulders. The father ran back to get a camera.

"Nice family," Jenny commented.

Chris shrugged. "All families look nice on the beach," he said.

"Gee, that wasn't *too* cynical," said Jenny. "What's *your* family like? Do you have any brothers or sisters?"

He shrugged a second time. "I'm an only child."

"Callie!" he heard the boy calling. "Come swim with me!"

He watched the boy pull the girl out of her mermaid cast, then grab a Boogie board and run to the water.

"Wait, Evan!" the girl called after him. "Wait for me!"

"What is it with her, anyway?" Chris asked.

"Her?" Jenny said. "She likes mermaids, I guess."

"Not her," said Chris. "The one back there on the steps. The one who watches me all the time."

Jenny glanced over her shoulder.

"Oh, her," she said. "I wouldn't get all paranoid, Chris. She's probably just terminally shy. Besides, aren't you used to being gawked at? I thought you hunky guys actually liked being sex objects."

"She doesn't look at me that way," said Chris. "She looks at me like she wants something."

"So why don't you ask her what she wants?"

Chris snorted. "Right," he said.

Turning his gaze back to the ocean, he began thinking about the previous summer when he'd been a guard on the other side of the island. He'd spent the whole time, practically, staring out over the bay at the sliver of New York in the distance, just wishing it could be a year later so he'd be finished with high school, working the beach side, and looking ahead to the rest of his life. Now here he was, and the rest of his life was as blank as the horizon.

Well, maybe not totally blank. He did have this plan. Right after Labor Day, he was going to start driving cross-country and not stop until he reached Malibu. He didn't know why Malibu, exactly, except he'd heard the surf was awesome. And it was three thousand miles away, a major point in its favor.

Destiny. That was the word for his plan. "California is my destiny," he liked to tell people. One time this girl said to him, "Don't you mean it's your *destination*?" That had really thrown him off, because *destination* made it all seem so small and unimportant. Hell, a destination was what you had when you went out for a six-pack or a pint of ice cream. But then he got *destiny* back in his head and his plan seemed big again.

After that, he was careful who he talked to about it. He knew the minute he'd met Jenny, who was in her third year at some fancy college majoring in psychology, of all things, that she was definitely *not* a likely candidate for this particular conversation, not if he didn't want to have his head messed with. Problem was, he seemed to be doing a fine job messing with his own head these days, didn't need Jenny or anybody else to do it for him.

One thing. He was glad to be away from home. No more having to listen to his mother getting on his case about not going to college or his old man saying, "Get off the kid's back. He's had his glory years. If I've told him once I've told him a hundred times, high school is as good as it gets."

Chris didn't like saying it, but his father was an asshole. Once, after they'd both knocked down a few brews (otherwise, he never would have had the guts), Chris asked his father, "What about Mom and me? Aren't *we* as good as it gets?" The old man hadn't answered, just muttered something Chris couldn't hear, not that he expected it amounted to much. Later on, his father had put his arm around Chris's shoulders and told him in this hot, slurry voice, "It's not that I don't love you and your mother." After his father pulled his arm away, Chris had stood there, squeezing his eyes shut, trying to imprint the moment on his memory because he was pretty sure he'd come about as close as he would ever get to hearing his father tell him he loved him. It would never get any better than that.

"I can't imagine what it's like being an only child," Chris heard Jenny say, "although sometimes I used to wish for it. I have two older sisters and a younger brother. Did you ever wish you had brothers or sisters?"

Chris shrugged. "Not really. What's the use of wishing?"

When Jenny didn't say anything, Chris fell into the silence between them and got lost in it. In no time at all, he was out there over the ocean again, floating, drifting, remembering . . .

Once there was a carpenter and this carpenter had a wife. They were only nineteen when they got married right out of high school, and it wasn't a year before they had a baby. Little blue-eyed boy named Michael. Michael Junior. After his daddy.

The carpenter had a workshop in the garage that was attached to his house, so he was home a lot, and that meant he could spend more time with his son than most fathers could.

He taught him his trade—as much as you could teach a boy of four—and he made up stories while they worked side by side. And whenever Michael the son put his hand in the way of danger, Michael the father pulled it away.

Then one day a couple of weeks before the boy's fifth birthday the father took him along on a job in a neighboring town.

"Now, Mikey," he told the boy when they got to the house, "I'm going to be working up on the roof today."

And Mikey said, "Let me go with you, Daddy. Please."

Well, the carpenter laughed at that, of course, because the boy was too little to have any business crawling around on a steep roof. No, he would never put his son in danger like that. "You go on now and play," he told Mikey. "There's a nice swing set in the yard. Play on that, and I'll be able to keep my eye on you."

From the roof, the father watched his son pumping away with his strong little legs, telling himself stories the way he always did. He saw him jump down off the swing to pet a dog that had wandered into the yard and he smiled, thinking how much his son loved dogs. *I'm going to get Mikey a dog for his birthday,* he thought, *that's what I'm going to do.*

Pleased with himself for coming up with such a clever idea, he went back to his work. *Gotta concentrate,* he told himself, *or I'll take one helluva spill and break my neck.* Pretty soon, he was so busy he didn't catch sight of the dog running off or little Mikey chasing after it. All he saw when he thought to check back and see how his son was doing was the motion of the empty swing.

The sharp cry of a seagull jarred Chris from his thoughts.

"What's the use of wishing?" he said.

"Did you say something?" Jenny asked.

Chris lowered his head. He didn't want to look out at the ocean anymore. He was tired of floating, tired of looking and not knowing what he was looking for.

"Chris?" Jenny said.

Chris raised his head and angled it slightly in Jenny's direction. "Nice day for fishing. That's all I said. Nice day for fishing. Unless, I guess, you're a fish."

Jenny laughed. Chris smiled at the sound of it. She was all right, Jenny was. She was the kind of person you could tell stuff to.

Maybe.

Maybe.

Angels burn with a heavenly fire. You must never touch them or get too close. Yet how the girl wished

how the girl yearned for the angel to lift her up and carry her in his arms across the waters of the sea to

to?

a land where she would be free

safe

to another land.

But what was the good of yearning for something that could never be?

But then one day the girl discovered that the angel was not the only one on the island. There was an entire kingdom filled with happy and loving people.

Each day the king and the queen would come to the seashore, and with them were the prince and the princess.

you can't always get
what you want

Callie stood beside her brother's bed. Glowing lime-green numbers told her it was 2:37. She was crying.

"I had a bad dream," she whispered in the dark.

Crawling into bed next to Evan, she said, "I'm thirsty." She smelled of tears and Johnson's Baby Shampoo.

"In a minute," her brother mumbled.

Whimpering, she said again, "I had a bad dream."

Evan rolled over and pulled his little sister close. "I know," he said. "But you're with me now. You're okay."

"We were all swimming. You and Mommy and Daddy and me, we were all swimming in the ocean. Then Mommy and Daddy weren't there, it was just you and me. I don't know where they went. Anyway." Callie licked her dry lips. "Anyway. We were swimming way, way out, so far out we couldn't see the beach anymore, but I heard the lifeguards calling, 'Come back, come back,' in these little voices, and I said, 'Let's keep going. Let's swim all the way home.' But I meant our real home, not the house here. And you said okay. Then I turned around and you weren't there anymore. I called out to you, but you didn't answer."

"Where was I?" Evan asked.

"I don't know. Just gone. Anyway. I thought you were coming back because I heard this splashing, but it wasn't you, it was this big, ugly monster. And he said, 'You're coming under the water with me, girlie.'"

"Girlie?" Evan laughed, and Callie said, "It isn't funny, Evan. It was very scary, for your stupid information."

"Sorry."

"So I said no, but he said I had to because it was his job. And the next thing I know he's pulling me under the water with these arms all covered with slimy seaweed and stuff. And I kept calling for you and Mommy and Daddy, but nobody came. And I was going under the water, and the monster was laughing. And that's when I woke up."

Evan stroked his sister's hair. "Monsters aren't real," he told her.

"Are, too."

"Okay. But I'd never let a monster take you anywhere."

"Monsters are bigger than you, Evan, and stronger. You couldn't save me from a monster."

"Could, too."

"But you couldn't save me from drowning."

"Could, too. I'd save you from anything, you know that. I'm not going to let anything hurt you."

"Honest?" Callie touched her tongue to a tear that had found its way to her lips.

"Honest."

She thought about it, then said, "I'm still thirsty."

As Evan got out of bed, Callie felt his

fuzzy leg brush hers. "Too bad you can't shave your legs the way girls do. I think it's disgusting that boys have hairy legs."

"Thank you very much," Evan said, and he left the room.

Callie watched the lime-green numbers and thought about how her brother had always been the one to bring her water in the middle of the night, to listen to her bad dreams. Evan said it wasn't true, it wasn't always like that, but as far as Callie was concerned it was. Evan told her it had started when she was four, after she came home from the hospital that time.

What she remembered was her brother reading to her while she ate strawberry Jell-O. Her jaw ached from where the cyst had been taken out, so she couldn't eat much and it hurt her to talk. And to laugh. Evan had tried to get her to laugh the minute she came home from the hospital as if he had decided it would be good medicine for her, and her first words to him were, "Stop it, Evan." Which he did, and that's when he started reading to her. He read to her every day when he got home from school, whatever books she wanted. He taught her how to make origami boxes, too, and birds.

One Saturday they watched the movie about the little mermaid, and she started wanting to be a mermaid, too. Every summer since then when they went to the beach, Evan had made her into a sand mermaid. One time they collected three whole buckets of shells and instead of making scales by marking her sand fin with the bottom of a pail, Evan covered the entire thing with tiny seashells. It had taken him almost an hour to do, and when he was finished Callie sat without moving for another hour, it felt like, so that all the people could stop and *ooh* and *aah* because they had never seen such a beautiful mermaid. Her legs hurt after a while, but she didn't complain because Evan had worked so hard. And, besides, she had never felt so much like a real mermaid in her life and she doubted she would ever feel that way again.

After Evan returned with a glass of water, Callie asked if she could stay in his bed with

him. The lime-green numbers glowing in the •
dark made her feel safe.

Evan said okay. He said okay about most
things, most of the time.

"Evan," Callie said after she had snuggled in,
"have you seen that girl watching us at the beach?"

Evan replied, his voice raw with fatigue, "Do
we have to talk about this now, Callie? I want to
sleep."

"You know what I think?" And then before
her brother could tell her he didn't care what
she thought, he just wanted to sleep, Callie said
in a hushed voice as if someone was outside the
door listening, "I think she's a spy."

"Kids can't be spies," Evan mumbled.

"Can, too," said Callie. "Harriet the spy is a spy."

"Harriet the spy is fiction. Now go to sleep."

Callie rolled down the corners of her mouth
as if Evan could see her, then turned on her side
to face the clock. It was 3:14. Drowsily, Callie
thought, *Three plus one equals four.* Her eyelids
drooped. "I still say she's a spy," she said, her voice
trailing off.

Evan heard, but didn't respond. He listened to her breathing grow slower and deeper. Soon she was sleeping and he was wide awake, aching for the summer night to envelop him in its warmth, to cradle him and rock him gently back to sleep. He heard in his head the line of that old Rolling Stones song, the one his father always sang to them in a mocking tone whenever he or Callie asked for the impossible, like an extra fifteen minutes in bed on a school morning or a third helping of ice cream, and the words mocked him now when all he was asking for was sleep: *You can't always get what you want, no, you can't always get what you want.*

His parents were always listening to rock, *their* rock. Hip music, his mother called it, because, she said, it was music you danced to with your hips when your hands were full, and she liked to play it when she washed the dishes. Before the sadness set in between his parents, his dad would come up behind his mom sometimes and lift her hands out of the soapy water, and they'd dance to the hip music together, his mother complaining that she was getting his shirt all wet and soapy and his father saying he liked it like that.

Evan thought how the sadness had been on his parents for a while now. If you didn't know better, say you were a dinner guest or something, you would never have suspected anything was different. But living in the house with them day after day the way he and Callie did, you couldn't help noticing all the little changes. The closed doors and the muffled voices. The red eyes. The way both his parents had to think before they smiled. The fact that maybe they still played their music, but the volume was lower and his father no longer liked to get his shirts wet and soapy.

The only other time Evan could remember like this was when Callie had been in the hospital. There were closed doors then, too, and muffled voices that got softer every time they came up against the word *cancer* (which it turned out Callie didn't have, after all), and when the doors opened, there were the red eyes and the delayed smiles. But the difference then was that his parents had been on the same side. Evan figured out that they were trying to protect him from their fears, which he didn't appreciate because he wasn't a baby, he was eleven, and he was scared his sister was dying and he didn't need protecting, he needed the truth and, for another thing, he needed his parents.

Evan sat up in bed. It was almost four o'clock. He listened to the crickets, or cicadas, or whatever they were, and found himself thinking about the girl who had been spying on them, to use Callie's words. He called her the watcher. He didn't know why, but there was something about her that bugged him. She had an attitude, he decided, always judging him. Always looking at him, thinking what a wuss he was, how he never went off and hung with the other guys but stuck to his family like glue, and she probably thought his family was so wonderful when any minute their parents' sadness could blow them apart like a hidden bomb.

In her room, Callie had this photograph of the four of them. It had been taken the previous summer by some guy who'd been walking along the beach when they'd stopped him and asked if he'd do them a favor. Evan remembered how funny the guy was, how he'd made them all laugh, and how the resulting photograph had captured more than four people standing there with their arms around one another. It had caught whatever it is that makes a family a family: not blood, not the love even, but the faith in itself, like it was a religion. Like it would always be there, going on forever.

A few months ago, Callie had taken the photograph from its spot on the mantel at home and put it on the nightstand by her bed. Her parents had never said a word about it. Nor did they say anything when she began putting it in her backpack to take with her to school each day. By the time they packed for their month at the beach house, it was understood that the photograph would be tucked away in Callie's suitcase, right next to her dolls and the stuffed animals she couldn't live without.

One time at home, Evan had gone into

Callie's bedroom and found her holding the photograph of the four of them in her left hand and another one—one their father had taken of the two children with their mother—in her right. "Before and after," Callie had said.

"Before and after what?" Evan had asked.

Callie had looked at him coolly. "The divorce, silly."

Evan didn't know if his parents were going to get divorced. He didn't know what had made them so sad. He only knew that Callie came to him most nights now with bad dreams, and that on some of those nights he had trouble falling back to sleep, and on some of *those* nights, now that they were out at the beach house, he lay awake and listened to the crickets or cicadas, or whatever they were, and sometimes he heard a dove cooing, and the sounds that filled his head were the saddest sounds in the universe, and he ached for the summer night to envelop him, to cradle him, to rock him gently back to sleep.

But you can't always get what you want.

Every day the girl would ask the doll to sing her song.

Flattered, the doll always said yes.

Once the doll was under the music's spell, the girl would steal the key from her pocket, sneak past the snoring beast, and be on her way to the kingdom she had discovered on the other side of the island.

One afternoon, she chanced to spy the prince reading a book. The queen was sitting nearby, and although there were common people all about, the prince and his mother were left to themselves.

The girl thought: He looks lonely, even if he is a prince.

Gathering all her courage, she approached the prince and spoke.

"Hello," she said, "I am

I am

I am

Miranda."

The queen looked up at the girl. "Miranda," she said softly. The girl wondered why she sounded so sad.

"I am Prince Evario," the boy said. "I have seen you before. I have been watching you."

This surprised the girl. "You have?" she said.

The prince nodded. "I was hoping you would come. You see, I could not come to you because I am the prince. Protocol, you know."

Miranda nodded, even though she did not understand. Not really.

"Now that you have come to me, however, we can be friends," said the prince. "Would you like that?"

"Oh, yes!" Miranda cried.

"So would I," said the prince.

The girl tried to remain calm, but inside she was shouting for joy.

one of these
very yellow guys

Evan hated Holden Caulfield. Really hated him. Maybe he was only a character in a book but to Evan he felt real, like one of those people you get stuck sitting next to on an airplane and they won't shut up about their totally unfascinating lives. Evan could in no way understand why his father had been shoving this book at him for the entire past year, insisting he read it, telling him it was one of the most important books of the twentieth century. His father got like that sometimes.

He decided to read it anyway. He'd seen it on his freshman reading list so he figured why not get it over with and get his father off his back at the same time. Two birds, one stone. In a weak moment, he'd admitted to his father that he hated Holden with a passion, and his father had given him this solemn look and said, "My guess is that this book is touching something deep inside you, Evan." To which he'd said, "Yeah, right, Dad." But sometimes in the middle of the night when he couldn't sleep, Evan wondered if maybe what his father said was true.

He was down at the beach reading the book one Friday afternoon when someone came up and said *hey* and asked if he wanted to hang out. It was Shane, one of what Evan referred to as the "boys in black." Evan often labeled people. He liked to think this was the product of a creative mind, but his best friend last year in eighth grade, right before he stopped being his best friend, had told Evan he thought he was basically a snob. Which Evan knew for a certifiable fact wasn't true, although no matter how many times he replayed the conversation in his head he couldn't come up with what he *was,* if he wasn't a snob.

The boys in black had caught Evan's attention the first week he and his family were out at the beach house. It was five o'clock, and like

every other day at five o'clock, after the lifeguards blew their whistles and waved their arms
to let everybody know they were going off duty,
little kids in bunches, Callie included, ran to the
abandoned lifeguard stand to clamber to the top,
hurl themselves off onto the huge pile of sand at
the base, then repeat the process over and over
until they were called away for dinner.

"Watch me, Evan!" Callie shouted. Evan
watched, at the same time keeping an eye on the
retreating figure of the lifeguard named Chris
who secretly Evan thought was the coolest guy
on the beach. Who secretly Evan wished he
could be. Evan admired Chris's mirrored sunglasses and had decided he was going over to Fair
Harbor one of these days to get a pair just like
them. The only question was whether he'd have
the nerve to wear them to the beach, although
he wasn't sure why this was even a question.

Evan was imagining himself sitting up on
top of the lifeguard stand in his mirrored sunglasses, twirling a whistle cord around his index
finger and looking seriously cool, when five

boys in black wet suits, shiny and snug as coats
of fresh paint, raced past and plunged into the
water. Once in, they pulled themselves onto
their surfboards and paddled furiously over
and through the rolling waves, calling to each
other all the while like crows cawing.
Everything about them worked together as
one: their bodies, their suits, their boards, the
water, their coded calls. Evan wished he could
be out there with them, envying not their
surfboards but their ease with themselves
and one another.

He saw them other times after that, other
places. Sometimes there'd be just one of
them, eating an ice cream out in front of the
all-purpose store in town, or two of them,
with fishing poles in hand, headed for the
bay. But most times he saw all five, moving
shoulder-to-shoulder along the boardwalks, a
basketball in constant play, looking, in their
high-style shorts and ankle bracelets and backward baseball caps, like a pack of Gap-ad
Huckleberry Finns.

At the beginning of their vacation his mother had been bugging him. "Why don't you make some friends, Evan? Those boys, you know the ones I mean, they look nice, don't you think?" He had come up with reasons, then excuses, and finally had just ignored his mother until she backed off.

Then there he was, hearing somebody say *hey,* and looking up at this tall, tightly muscled kid with shoulder-length dirty-blond hair whom he recognized immediately as the one he'd heard the others call Shane.

"I see you sittin' here," Shane said, squinting down at Evan. "How come you're always sittin' here reading?"

"I'm not always reading."

"I never see you in the water."

"I go in the water. Maybe not when you're looking."

Evan's cheeks were hot. He prayed that his mother, stretched out on a towel several feet behind him, was plugged into her music or one of those meditation tapes she was always listening to these days and wasn't paying attention to this conversation.

"So what's your name?" he heard Shane ask.

"Evan. What's yours?"

"Shane," Shane said in a bored voice. "So you want to hang out? I mean, you know, you want to hang out?"

"I guess," Evan said. His eyes were level with Shane's knees. He noticed now many pink scars and scabs dotted the landscape of the other boy's sun-brown legs. He imagined all the falls and mishaps it must have taken to create so many scars and felt a deep sense of shame that at fourteen his own body revealed so little history.

"Where's the rest of, you know . . ." Evan raised his eyes and let his question fall away.

Shane shrugged. "Josh and Eric had to go home for a few days. Brendan's *bonding* with his stepdad, for godsake, he's like, I just want to take *you* sailing, Brendan, none of your friends this time, okay? I mean, like, that's really gonna win points with Brendan, right?"

Evan nodded sympathetically.

"So, anyway, Joel and me, we were gonna hang together, but then he had to do this thing with his sister. Anyway, where's your sister at? For a long time, I thought maybe you were like a hired *baby*-sitter or something, the way you were always with her, playing and everything, y'know."

Embarrassed and flattered at the same time, Evan stammered, "I, uh, she's, she's with a friend, she made a friend, she's at her friend's house."

"Oh." Impatiently, Shane ran a self-admiring hand over his shirtless chest. "So?" he said.

"Sure," Evan said, rising to his feet. He turned to look down at his mother, whose approving smile at once granted him permission to leave and acknowledged that she had heard everything.

As they were leaving the beach, the girl who sat on the top of the steps, the one Evan called the watcher, quickly closed the book in which she was writing and ran off.

"Cereal material," Shane muttered contemptuously.

"Huh?"

"The girl's a flake," said Shane. He turned to Evan and arched his eyebrows.

"I guess," Evan said.

"Not to mention that she's like a public *nuisance,* sitting there all the time, blocking traffic. Somebody ought to do something about her.

"Hey, I'm hungry," he continued as they left the beach and Evan puzzled over the veiled threat in Shane's words. "You hungry?"

"I guess," Evan said. "Sure."

"You like pizza? They got the *best* pizza over in Fair Harbor. Who doesn't like pizza, right? You wanna split one?"

"Sure," Evan said again. It was just occurring to him to wonder why Shane had taken this sudden interest in him.

Coming to a long row of haphazardly parked bicycles, Shane asked, "You got wheels?"

Indicating that he did, Evan retrieved the rust-eaten dirt bike he'd claimed as his the day he and his family had moved into the rental house. Most houses on the island came with bikes; cars weren't allowed, so if you wanted to get any-where fast a two-wheeler was the only way.

The trip to Fair Harbor was a short one, under five minutes if there weren't too many walkers or joggers clogging the narrow walkways. Since it was easier to go single file, Evan let Shane take the lead, which gave him a chance to think about what was happening. The funny thing was that for as long as he'd been watching the boys in black he'd been putting them down in his head and at the same time wishing he could be one of them. When Shane came over and asked him to hang out, it was as if a movie star had just invited him to be in his new movie. But even though Evan had jumped at the invitation like a hungry dog going for a handout, he wasn't sure he even *liked* Shane, much less wanted to be in a movie with him. One thing was for sure: the whole situ-ation was making him nervous.

As they got closer to Fair Harbor, Shane pointed off to his right. "My house is down that street," he shouted. "Second in from the beach." The island was so narrow at this point you could stand in the middle and easily see the sea on one side and the bay on the other. Evan looked to see if he could make out which house was Shane's but was distracted by the loud music coming from one of the houses at the bay end of the same street. He was pretty sure it was opera, though he couldn't have told you which one. The thing about it was, you didn't expect to hear that kind of music out at the beach. Yet in a funny sort of way it fit. At least, to Evan it did. It made him think of other island sounds: the doves cooing in the middle of the night, the cicadas, the plaintive foghorns. They were lonely sounds. This was a lonely sound, too.

When he said something to Shane about it later, Shane told him that the people who lived in that house were probably deaf. "For real," he said. "They've played that music so loud the police have had to come a coupla times to get 'em to turn it down. If you ask me you'd *have* to be deaf to listen to that shit anyway. Shit sounds like a bunch of cats gettin' their *balls* yanked. If you ask me."

After they got their pizza, they carried it to the end of the ferry dock and, over sodas and wedges, swapped "stats," as Shane put it. Shane lived in New York City; Evan in a small town on the Hudson River just north of the city. Shane went to private school; Evan to public. Both were starting high school in the fall. Shane had two brothers, one in college, one just married. Evan had a sister, going into second grade.

To Evan, the most interesting thing about Shane was the one thing Shane didn't want to talk about. His parents had been recently divorced. As part of the settlement, his mother had gotten the apartment on Central Park West and the house on the island. She had also gotten Shane.

When Evan asked, "So what's it like?" Shane asked back, "What's what like?"

And when Evan said, "Having divorced parents," Shane shrugged and said, "It's like having divorced parents."

Case closed.

Shane switched the subject to sports, which

didn't interest Evan that much, and then to girls. Which is to say, to sex—a topic that inspired Shane and made Evan itchy. Most of the time, Evan had only a vague idea of what Shane was talking about but was too embarrassed to let on. Which Shane quickly figured out.

"So did you ever do *that* with a girl?" he asked Evan at one point, his eyes daring him to lie.

"Not exactly," Evan said.

Shane snorted. "What d'ya mean, not exactly? You've either done it or you haven't. You probably haven't even *kissed* a girl. Tell the truth."

Evan felt his throat tighten, his cheeks burn. A picture flashed into his mind of himself shoving Shane, hard, into the bay. He imagined Shane hitting his head on a rock and water filling his lungs as he, Evan, went off slowly to seek help.

"No," he heard himself say.

"Geez," Shane said, "you sure thought about it long enough." He jabbed Evan lightly on the arm. "No big deal. City boys grow up faster than small-town boys. It's a known fact."

Shane didn't wait for Evan's response. He stood up and stretched lazily; then, in a different voice than Evan had heard him use before, he said, "Hey, you got pockets?"

Evan looked up at him. "Pockets?"

"Pockets. You know, pockets."

"Oh. Yeah. I got pockets."

Shane smiled. "Great. Let's have some fun."

"But what—"

"What do you need?"

"What do I need?"

"Or want. What do you want? Let's see." Shane bent down to scoop up the empty pizza box with one hand, indicating to Evan that he should take care of the soda cans. "Like, for example, I could use a new lure."

"Oh," Evan said. "Well, I've been wanting to get some sunglasses."

"Shades," Shane said. "Perfecto."

They dumped their garbage in the can outside the general store. Shane turned to Evan, dropping his voice to a near whisper. "Two rules. First, you gotta ask for what you want. Then after you take it, you gotta say somethin' on your way out like, 'I didn't see anything I liked.' Or, uh, 'Thanks, anyway. Maybe next time.' Got it?"

"What do you mean, *take* it?" Evan asked.

"What d'ya *think* I mean?"

"Steal?"

Shane clapped a hand on Evan's shoulder. "Brilliant," he said. "Now, come on. Shades are an *excellent* choice, by the way, a *total* challenge for the advanced player. They're right up by the register."

As Shane dropped his hand away, Evan said, "But we don't need to steal. This stuff doesn't cost much. Besides, we can just charge it to our parents' accounts. I don't get why—"

Shane turned back, losing patience. "Listen, turkey," he said. "We don't *need* to do anything, right? That's the point. It's a question of creating a little entertainment value, okay? So you with me or what?"

Evan despised himself for knowing without

having to think about it what his answer would be. "I'm with you," he said.

"My *man*," said Shane, holding out his hand for Evan to slap him five.

The store had only a handful of customers when the boys entered. Two girls leafing through magazines glanced up at Evan and Shane to see if they were worth more than a glance. A mother, with a child in a stroller, was in the hardware section.

"You ever done this before?" Shane whispered. "Never mind, I don't wanna know. Just keep alert to where everybody is and where they're looking. And *don't* act suspicious. And *don't* look at me, just concentrate on what you're doing. Anyway, we're lucky. It looks like there's only one person working. And she's a total airhead."

A girl of eighteen or so was wiping down the counter at the front of the store. Her hand was just inches away from the rack of sunglasses.

"Don't forget the rules," Evan heard Shane

whisper before he walked brazenly up to the girl and asked, " 'Scuse me, you got any fishing lures?"

The girl's eyes narrowed slightly when she looked into Shane's face. Evan wondered if she recognized him and had guessed what he was up to. But then she said as casually as she would say to anybody asking anything, "Yeah, sure, they're back there with the sports stuff behind hardware."

Evan knew it was his turn now, but how was he supposed to ask where the sunglasses were when they were staring right at him?

The girl gave the plastic bottle in her right hand a squeeze, then began to wipe the countertop. "You need help with something?" she asked, looking Evan's way.

"Um, yes," Evan said. "Sunglasses are . . . those sunglasses there, are they the only ones you've got?"

The girl said, "That's it," and went on with her cleaning.

Evan approached cautiously, turning back

only when he heard the girls at the magazines whispering. The palms of his hands were practically dripping they were so sweaty all of a sudden.

Turning the display rack, he began to hope he wouldn't see the glasses he wanted. After all, why should he steal a pair he *didn't* want? He could just tell Shane . . . what? That he couldn't do it? Evan began coming up with a plan. He'd steal a pair of glasses, any pair, the cheaper the better. Then he'd come back another time, alone, and, just the way he'd taken them when no one was looking, he'd put them back when no one was looking.

Now that his conscience was eased, all he had to do was "borrow" them without getting caught. He gave the rack another turn and spotted the ones he wanted. From the looks of it, they were the only pair left. What if he took them and quietly said to the girl, "Charge, please," and hoped that Shane didn't hear?

"Excuse me." Evan and the girl both looked back toward the hardware section. "Can you help me?" the mother with the baby asked.

"I'm having trouble finding what I'm looking for."

Putting her bottle and rag down on the counter, the girl said to Evan, "I'll be right back," and left him alone with the sunglasses. Lifting them gingerly from the rack, he put them on and studied himself in the mirror. He looked older, tougher. More like Chris.

"I couldn't find what I wanted. Thanks, anyway."

Evan turned at the sound of Shane's voice and watched him sauntering up the aisle past the salesgirl. As he went by Evan, he patted his pocket and winked.

Evan looked around. No one was paying any attention to him. Wiping his hands on his bathing suit, he carefully took off the sunglasses, folded them, and told himself he could do it. He *could*. He could slip them into his pocket. He could even come back another time and pay for them. Shane would never need to know that part of it. He just needed to see Evan come out of the store, patting his pocket.

A burst of laughter jarred him from his thoughts. Coming through the door with a bunch of his buddies was Chris, wearing the same kind of sunglasses Evan held in his hands. Chris looked right at him, or Evan thought he did, so taking him by surprise that he thrust the sunglasses under a pile of goggles and nose-guards that were sitting in a box on the counter. He rushed out of the store, remembering only at the last minute to call back in a faltering voice, "I couldn't, I didn't find what I wanted."

"My *man!*" Shane cried when they'd rounded the corner to fetch their bikes. "Lemme see. Where are they?"

"I, I had them in my hands," Evan stammered, "but I couldn't—"

Shane cut him off. "Forget it," he said. "Listen, it's almost five-thirty. I've gotta meet the ferry back in Saltaire."

"But I can explain," Evan said. "I was going to do it. Honest. See, what happened—"

Shane put his hand on Evan's shoulder, but it felt different this time, less like a buddy, more like a teacher who's pulled you aside to have a serious talk. "Don't sweat it, okay? It was just for a goof. Don't make a federal *case* out of it.

"Anyway, I gotta meet that ferry. You comin' or what?"

Evan nodded, mounting his bike and trailing behind Shane. The whole way back, Evan tried not hating himself, tried telling himself that he'd done the right thing, that it was Shane who should be feeling bad about what he'd done, not *him* for what he hadn't. He imagined himself saying all sorts of things to Shane, but none of them changed the way he pictured Shane responding—the patronizing touch on the shoulder, the look in the eyes telling him he had failed.

They arrived just in time for the five-thirty ferry. Shane, with barely a backward glance, dropped his bike and called out, "There's my main man! There's Josh!"

Evan saw a boy waving from the top deck of the ferry. "Yo, bud!" he heard the boy call out. Then he heard, "Evan!" And for a moment he imagined that Josh, who didn't even know him, was calling his name.

But it was his father who was calling, his father who clapped his hand on Evan's shoulder as they walked back to their house, his father who said, "Well, this is a nice surprise. I didn't know you'd be meeting me at the ferry."

Evan said, "I guess I missed you, Dad," as Shane passed them on his bike, balancing his main man Josh on the crossbar.

"See you, Shane!" Evan called out, with a sideways glance at his father.

Shane didn't answer, just cocked his head slightly to indicate he'd heard.

"Another surprise," Evan's father said. "You've made some friends."

"I guess," said Evan.

That night, out on their screened-in porch, as his mother and sister played Uno and his father muttered his way through a crossword puzzle, Evan picked up *The Catcher in the Rye* and tried reading again the part of the book where Holden calls himself a coward. "One of these very yellow guys," was how he put it, and those words were one of the biggest reasons Evan hated Holden Caulfield.

He's a loser, Evan thought, shutting the book and looking down at his long, fuzzy, scarless legs. *A total loser.*

In the days that followed, the girl and the prince spent much of their time together. They loved to walk along the beach, collecting shells and talking. Miranda thought the prince the most perfect companion she could imagine. She dared not tell him so, but then he surprised her by saying, "You are the best friend I've ever had, Miranda. I feel as if we have known each other always."

"Perhaps we have," Miranda replied.

They looked into each other's eyes, wondering.

The girl noticed that the prince never told her how he and his family came to rule the island. In like manner, he never asked her where she lived or where she went at each day's end. She was glad for that for she could never have told him about the beast and the enchanted doll.

The princess was named Caliandra. She adored the older girl, telling her, "You are the sister I always wished I had. Not that my brother isn't kind, but there is something special between sisters, don't you agree?"

The girl did not know how to answer, for she had never had a sister. But in her heart she believed that what the princess said was true, and almost told her, "I wish you were my sister."

One day as Miranda helped Caliandra build a sand castle, the princess asked, "What is that locket you wear about your neck?"

Miranda touched the golden locket and felt her heart grow heavy. "It was a birth gift from my mother," she said. "I lost her long ago. I have no memory of her, only this locket."

Caliandra took the locket in her tiny fingers. It was a heart, or rather a piece of one, for it looked as if a jagged saw had cut the heart down the middle and left only half. It was odd to behold, but odder yet was the truth now dawning on the young princess.

"I have seen another such locket," said Caliandra excitedly. "Perhaps it is the mate to this one."

"But where?" asked Miranda.

Caliandra leaned over to whisper in Miranda's ear. "Amongst my mother's possessions," she said.

a perfect day for flying

"My parents are getting divorced," Callie said, trying the words on for size. They felt a little loose, but it wasn't impossible that she'd grow into them in time.

Sarah looked over the top of the sand castle she and Callie were building. "Really?" she asked solemnly.

Callie nodded matter-of-factly. "I'm going to stay in our house with my mother," she said. "My brother Evan has to move out and live with my father."

"They're going to split you up?" Sarah put down her shovel to give this disturbing thought her full attention. "That's really mean. Unless, I guess, unless you don't *like* your brother, then I guess it's okay."

"Oh, I like my brother," Callie said, checking

out of the corner of her eye to see if Sarah's mother, sitting under a nearby umbrella, was listening. Seeing that she was occupied reading to Sarah's little sister, Callie dared to proceed.

"It's not fair, but what can you do?" She shrugged. "We're just kids, they don't care about us."

"But they're your parents," Sarah argued. She began to rock back and forth on her haunches, feet splayed, arms tightly wound around her knees. Callie leaned across their half-finished castle and pushed Sarah's glasses, which were forever slipping, up to the bridge of her nose. Callie and Sarah had been friends for three days. They had already worn each other's bathing suits; they were accustomed to familiarity.

"I *told* you it wasn't fair," Callie said, sounding impatient but not feeling it. She was surprised how quickly she was growing into her story, how the words were starting to fit.

"But *why?*" Sarah asked. She too glanced over at her mother, not to see if she was listening but to be sure she was there. "Why are they getting a divorce?"

Callie thought. "They're tired of each other, I guess. You know how you have a favorite doll and you think if you ever lose her you'll die?"

Sarah nodded; her glasses slipped.

"But then you get a new doll for your birthday or something?"

"Christmas," said Sarah.

"Or Chanukah," said Callie because that was her holiday. "Anyway, so now this new doll is your favorite and you don't care about the old one anymore and you could even give her away if you had to."

"I could *never* give one of *my* dolls away," Sarah said passionately. "I don't care if she wasn't my favorite anymore. I just couldn't."

"Oh, I know. I could never, either. But, just *say* you could, okay? It's like that with my parents, see?" Callie scooped up a handful of sand. "Understand?"

"I *don't* understand," Sarah said. "How do you know the old doll isn't going to be your favorite again? I mean, you never know, right? That's happened to me lots of times." She picked up her shovel and began furiously to dig.

"Hey," Callie said, "you're getting sand on me."

"Sorry."

Adding her handful of sand to the pile Sarah was rapidly building up, Callie said, "You're lucky your parents aren't getting divorced."

Sarah said, "I don't know *anybody* whose parents are getting divorced."

"You're lucky," Callie said.

"How many towers are we going to have?" Sarah asked.

"I don't know. Seven?"

Sarah smiled. "That's *perfect*," she said. "It's like us. Get it? We're seven years old: seven towers. Get it?"

"Yeah," Callie said happily. "Seven: seven."

Sarah ran to get her best plastic tower mold, which had somehow found its way into her little sister's hands, as Callie, patting a mound of sand, gazed past her friend to the girl sitting on the wooden steps in the distance. The girl seemed to be looking at her, too, but they were so far apart Callie couldn't tell for certain.

"Did you ever read *Harriet the Spy?*" Callie asked Sarah when she returned. Sarah was being trailed by her sister Irene, who was wailing and grabbing for the sand toy.

"Sarah, you mustn't just *take!*" Sarah's mother yelled at her.

"*Me* want!" demanded Irene.

"My dad read it to me," Sarah said, pushing aside her sister's sandy little paws.

"*No-o-o!*" Irene shrieked.

"Sarah!"

"I didn't just *take* it!" Sarah called over her shoulder.

"Well, that's her," said Callie.

"Who?"

"Harriet the spy, that's what I'm telling you."

"Where?"

"I can't point because she's watching us, but if you turn very slowly and pretend you're looking for something, there's a girl sitting on the steps over there and that's Harriet the spy."

"Me-e-e!" Irene screeched.

"Let her play with you!" Sarah's mother shouted. "Sarah, do you *hear* me?"

"I *am!*" Sarah called, giving Irene the evil eye.

Sarah turned to look where Callie had instructed her. She shaded her eyes with one hand. "I don't see—oh, *that* girl? She's there all the time."

"Well, that's Harriet the spy."

"You said that."

"But I'm *telling* you," said Callie with such confidence it didn't occur to Sarah to contradict her.

"I didn't know she was real," Sarah said, handing Irene a toy the younger girl didn't want. "I thought that story was made up."

Callie said, "It is, but it's based on a real girl. And that's her."

"Wow," Sarah said as the two girls began digging a moat and Irene found peace with the new toy, which turned out to be more intriguing than a tower mold. "That is so cool.

I wish I could be like her. You know: spy on people, write stuff down. You think she looks in people's windows and everything?"

"Of course," Callie said. "She's Harriet."

The girls worked in silence until Sarah said softly, "I wonder if she's writing about *us*."

Callie looked up, meeting her friend's eyes, and the two girls began to giggle.

"Why are we laughing?" Sarah asked.

"I don't know," Callie said.

Returning to her work, Callie imagined:

There are these two girls on the beach. One of them has straight red hair and glasses and a bratty little sister named Irene. The other one has brown hair and freckles like her mother. That one, the one with brown hair and freckles, is a big liar who makes up stories. Like about her parents getting divorced, which who knows if it's even going to happen, and me being Harriet the spy when everybody knows that book is made up and I'm a real girl.

All of a sudden Callie wondered just who the girl *was,* if she wasn't Harriet the spy. It wasn't long, however, before the effort of building their sand castle took all her concentration, and the girl in the distance, the girl Evan called the watcher, faded away in Callie's mind to a ghost of a thought. There, but invisible. And after a while Callie forgot her altogether so that the girl became nothing, not even a ghost, not even there.

When her brother and parents arrived on the beach, Callie ran to meet them, eager to show off the completed sand castle.

"We worked on it *all* morning!" she crowed.

"*Both* of us!" Sarah said. "*I* made the bridge."

Tugging on Evan's hand, Callie said breathlessly, "We can't decide whether we should call it Castle Saracal or Castle Callisar. What do *you* think, Evan?"

Looking down at his sister's—and her new best friend's—eager faces, Evan said, "That's a pretty important decision."

"It is," Callie agreed seriously.

"*I* know," said Sarah, "let's take a—what do you call that, when you ask lots of people the same question?"

"A poll?" Evan asked.

"It starts with an *s*," said Sarah, shaking her head.

"A survey," said Evan.

"A survey, that's it."

"Good idea," said Callie. "*I* know. Let's collect shells and stones. Then we'll take two buckets. Everyone who wants Castle Saracal will put a stone in the stone bucket, and everyone who wants Castle Callisar will put a shell in the shell bucket."

Propelled by their own cleverness and the importance of their mission, the two girls raced off, leaving Evan to shake his head at the way seven-year-old minds worked.

"What do you say?" he heard his father ask. "Shall we launch this thing? It's a perfect day for flying a kite."

Evan turned to see his father holding the kite he had brought back with him from the "mainland," as he insisted on calling it. It was a beauty, there was no denying it. A delta kite with long silvery streamers trailing off its three points. On its back was the image of an imaginary bird, handpainted in brilliant colors: turquoise and silver, purple and orange, bright, bright yellow.

When it was airborne it was unlike any other kite in the sky. It shimmered and swooped, and the way the silver caught the sun it seemed to burst into tiny flames, to dance with silver shoes.

Although his father had launched it, it was Evan who now held the spool, Evan who felt the tug of the wind as he let out or took in the line.

"That's it, give it a little more now," he heard his father coaching from a few feet behind him.

"I *know* what I'm doing," Evan said, even though he didn't really. At least, his mind didn't. His body seemed to know *exactly* what it was doing. He couldn't remember ever feeling so connected to something outside himself. It was as if he and the kite were one. As if *he* were flying.

"I want a turn," he heard Callie say.

"In a minute," he told her.

"Please," Callie pleaded. "It's not fair."

"It's not fair," Sarah echoed. "Please, Evan!"

He looked down, first at Sarah, then at his sister, who had a glint in her eye that told him she knew she had already won.

"Hold it *with* me," he instructed them.

As Callie and Sarah jostled for a position next to Evan and ended up on either side of him, Evan felt Irene brushing against his legs.

"Me-e-e!" she whined.

Evan laughed. "You, too?"

"Me, too."

"Well, I don't know, can somebody—" Looking over at his parents, Evan was surprised to see that his father had his arm around his mother's shoulders and she was just then putting her arm around his waist. They smiled at him, easily, the way they used to smile before they had to think about it.

"Can somebody put Irene on my shoulders?" Evan continued.

"Oh, let me," said her mother.

She rushed forward and lifted Irene up. As Evan felt the child's soft, sandy thighs grip his neck and her arms wrap themselves tightly around the crown of his head, he kept an eye on his parents and was relieved that they had not removed their arms from each other's bodies. He said a silent, a quick, an unconscious prayer, and breathed out, realizing when he did that he'd been holding his breath.

"Oh, *look* at you kids," Sarah's mother gushed. "Don't anybody move, I'm just going to get my camera, if I can only . . ."

She hurried off to dig in her beach bag. Irene bounced on Evan's shoulders as Sarah muttered, "My mother takes a kazillion pictures."

"I like pictures," Callie told her friend. "I like having them."

"Me, too," said Sarah, "but who needs a kazillion?"

"Evan," Callie said, "would you ask Sarah's mom to take a picture of Mommy and Daddy?"

"I thought you said your parents were getting divorced," Sarah whispered to Callie, loud enough that Evan heard. "They don't *look* like they're getting divorced."

"I said they *might* be getting divorced," Callie hissed.

"Did not," said Sarah. "You said—"

"Everybody look over here!"

Evan smiled, tickling the soles of Irene's feet so that she was laughing when the shutter clicked.

"One more! Nobody blink! And, Sarah, don't make rabbit ears behind Callie this time!"

Callie and Sarah poked each other from either side of Evan's legs and giggled.

As the second picture was being taken, Evan heard someone call his name. "Evan, yo, Evan! Awesome kite, man!"

He turned his head in the direction of the voice, and there were the boys in black, standing at the water's edge, watching him fly his kite. His awesome kite.

"Hold on tight! Don't let it go now!" he warned the girls as he took a hand away from the spool to wave to Shane.

Shane waved back. He yelled something Evan couldn't hear.

"What?" Evan shouted.

"Check out the flake!" Indicating that Evan should look behind him, Shane called out again, "The *flake!*"

Awkwardly, Evan turned his head to look where Shane was pointing. There, on the top of the steps where she usually sat, the watcher stood with her arms stretched out wide, her back arched, her head lifted to the sky.

"She's flying!" Evan called back to Shane.

"She's crazy!" Shane returned.

Evan shook his head no. "She's flying," he said again, not quite so loudly this time, because he was flying, too, and he didn't want Shane or his gang spoiling anyone's fun. Not his, not the watcher's. *It's a perfect day for flying,* he thought to himself.

Giving the little girl's foot a squeeze, he said, "Right, Irene?"

Irene squealed. And Evan took it to mean, *Right, Evan.*

●

The queen held her locket up next to the girl's. The two halves fit perfectly.

The queen began to cry. "When you said your name was Miranda, I . . . I did not dare hope . . . Miranda. We thought she had drowned when she was a baby. When we were shipwrecked off the shores of this island . . ."

The queen could control her crying no more. She left off her speech, and the king went on.

"I held both my babies to my chest as I attempted to swim to safety," he explained. "But it was a stormy sea that day, and a sudden wave knocked one of my children out of my arms. I did not know which one it was. I called out, Evario! Miranda! But I heard no cry, only the roar of the angry sea fighting to take my other child away from me."

Miranda looked at Evario. "Then you are . . ."

"Your brother," said Evario. "Your twin."

The girl fell into her long-lost brother's arms. Caliandra hugged her, too. "At last, I have a sister,"

Caliandra said. *"A real sister."*

"Yes," said Miranda. *And to the prince she said, "And so it is true that we have always known each other."*

Alas, Miranda's happiness was but brief.
For she knew she must return each night to the beast. His powers were too great, too strong
    too magical
    to be resisted. If he discovered her with her true family, he would destroy her
    he would destroy them all.

ain't nobody's business

Around the third week of August, God turned up the thermostat. Chris took it personally: punishment for his sins.

"Never again," he mumbled, "as God is my witness."

"Yeah, right," said Jenny. "I wouldn't bring God into it, if I were you, Chris. She might take a dim view of your leisure-time activities, if you get my drift."

"No, I swear, Jenny, I am *never* going to party like that again. It's, it's sick, y'know?"

"Oh, *I* know. And you know, too. The problem is, by tonight you'll be back in your blessed state of ignorance. Tabula rasa."

Chris turned slowly to face Jenny. He couldn't stand when she pulled that college crap on him. "What's that supposed to mean?" he asked.

" 'Blank slate,' " said Jenny. "Hey, you may hate my intelligence, but no more than I hate your stupidity."

"That's mighty Christian of ya," Chris said.

"I didn't mean it like that. I only meant I hate it because I know it's an act. I mean, you're a lot more, you've got more . . . oh, never mind what I mean. I'm sorry I said anything."

Chris turned back to face the ocean, feeling his neck crack as he did.

"I'm not stupid," he said.

"That's just what I'm saying."

"Yeah. Well."

"Anyway," Jenny said, reaching down to pick up the bottle of water at her foot, "it's none of my business what you do with your life."

"Ain't nobody's business."

"Huh?"

"It's a song."

"Oh."

"Can't remember what it's called," said Chris. "Maybe just that. Ain't nobody's business."

"Fine."

"Anyway, there's this party over at Kelly and her housemate's, what's-her-name, tonight. In Kismet. You going?"

Jenny sighed. "I suppose," she said. "But I'm not drinking. And neither should you. Look at you, what if somebody gets in serious trouble out there today? Are you going to be able to—"

"Will you please shut the hell up?" Chris snapped. "I'm in no shape for a lecture from Mother Teresa right now, okay?"

"Fine." Jenny took a swig of water and muttered something Chris couldn't make out.

Chris thought, *This must be what it's like to be married. Thinking you got a right to tell somebody else how to live their life. And maybe the other person just doesn't want to hear it, okay? Maybe they just need to work things out on their own. Shit. Why do I feel like I should be apologizing? For what? I didn't ask for her opinion. And anyway she's the one calling me stupid. Am I right?*

Chris glanced at his watch. It was eleven-thirty. The beach wasn't all that crowded, which was a surprise considering the weather. He looked around for the regulars. The mermaid girl was off to his left, playing in the sand with her friend with the red hair. The little one, the friend's sister, was curled up on a blanket, sacked out in the shade of her mother's umbrella. He envied her. To be able to pass out like that in the hot sun, sleep deep, no worries. What did Jenny call it? Blank something. Tabula something.

The two moms were sitting close to each other in beach chairs, talking. The boy, the mermaid's brother, was stretched out on a towel on his side, propped up on an elbow, a book in his hand. Chris noticed that the boy had new sunglasses, the same as his. He wasn't sure why he got a kick out of that, but he did.

He wondered where the father was. He was usually around, or at least he was around more than most of the fathers who showed up late on Friday afternoons and were gone by Sunday. He thought about what he'd said to Jenny that time about all families looking nice on the beach. He didn't know why he said stuff like that, all sarcastic-like, because the fact of the matter was, this family *did* look nice. They were always doing things together, then taking pictures of themselves doing it. Not that lots of families didn't do that, but there was just something—he didn't know how to describe it. He didn't have the words. They never yelled at each other, was that it? And the brother, he actually seemed to *like* his kid sister. Take the time he was flying that kite, the way he let her and her friend help out and popped the little one up on his shoulders. That was really something.

But that wasn't it either, exactly. What *was* he trying to get at?

Maybe, Chris thought, *maybe I am stupid, maybe it's not an act.*

"I don't know," Chris said. "Half the time I don't even want to go to these parties, y'know?"

"I know what you mean," Jenny said, the flatness of her tone encouraging Chris to continue.

"It's not, I'm not stupid, but sometimes I just don't even know who I am. Okay, that sounds crazy, but it's like, that party last night.

I get a little high, okay, and there's so many people, and loud music, and everybody's sweaty and drunk, and shouting at everybody because nobody can hear you if you don't shout. Sometimes, you can't even tell if *you're* the one shouting or, or, *where* you are anymore, because everybody's dancing and moving at the same time, all packed together and shouting, and it's like one big, one big . . ."

Chris was sweating. He wiped his forehead with the palm of his hand.

"One big animal," said Jenny.

"That's it, that's what I mean. It's like you're just a part of one big animal and you keep moving and shouting and drinking and doing whatever you do because that's what the animal does and you're just part of it. And, and, that's when you think: I'm not *stupid,* but sometimes it's like I don't have a brain, y'know? I'm just a part of the animal, and not the *thinking* part. That's what I hate, y'know? That's what—"

Chris caught a droplet of sweat on his tongue. Its sour taste made him want to curl up somewhere and fall asleep for a good long time.

"You look awful," Jenny said. "I mean it, you look really low."

"Mighty Christian of—"

"Craig! Cover for Chris, will ya? He's not doing so good."

"Maybe I *should* lie down," Chris said.

"Go back to the house," Jenny advised.

"I can go under the tarp. I'll lie down under the tarp."

"No," Jenny said in a no-nonsense voice. "Go back to the house and get some real sleep. You lie out in this heat, you're going to feel even sicker when you get up."

Craig's head appeared at the top of the ladder. He took one look at Chris and said, "You make shit look good."

"Very nice," Chris said. But he didn't need further convincing. His head was killing him. He'd already taken four aspirins or some kind of damn pain pills, whatever they were; one of his housemates had given them to him, and he knew he shouldn't take any more for another couple of hours at least. Maybe sleep would help, maybe he'd just let Jenny and Craig and the rest of them take over, and he'd sack out. All afternoon. And tonight he'd go easy. No heavy stuff. He wouldn't let himself become part of the animal.

As he made his way toward the steps leading away from the beach (the sand burning the soles of his feet), he noticed the girl sitting there in her usual spot, watching him. She was looking right at him, like she didn't think he could see her sitting there staring. She didn't avert her eyes until Chris was practically standing right next to her.

And then, he didn't know what made him do it, he stopped and he said to her, "You okay?"

He was looking at the top of her head now. She'd hunched her shoulders up and pushed her head over to the side, out of Chris's way, as soon as he'd stepped foot on the bottom stair. She was all bunched up over that little notebook she was always writing in, protecting it, or herself, or who knows what.

"I mean it," Chris said gently. "You okay?"

The girl didn't move. Chris noticed she had a number of nasty-looking mosquito bites all red and raw on her arms and legs.

"You shouldn't pick at those," he told her. "I'm talkin' about those bites there. You gotta let 'em scab over, let 'em heal up."

She said nothing. He tried another tack.

"Hey, how come you sit up here all the time, huh? Why don't you come down on the beach and have some fun? You swim?"

The girl lifted her head slightly. Chris waited for a response, but a sudden stab of pain behind his eyes sent a wave of nausea through him. He had to lie down.

"I gotta go," he said to the girl as if he were interrupting her in the middle of a sentence. "Okay? You gonna be okay?"

Still, no response. Chris shrugged. He hoped Jenny wasn't watching. Last thing he wanted her thinking was that he was moving in on her territory as Mother Teresa or anything like that.

He was almost at the bike rack before he turned around. He wasn't surprised to see the girl looking at him over her shoulder. What he wasn't prepared for were her eyes. It was like they were screaming, like they were burning up on fire, and somebody was behind them, inside there, screaming to get out. Chris thought maybe he was dreaming, maybe he was so sick he was standing there with people passing by, with their towels and folding chairs and Boogie boards, and he was right there in the middle of all of them having a dream. And it was about this girl whose eyes were on fire, and there was somebody trapped inside, screaming.

"Man," Chris said, wiping away the sweat that was drenching his forehead. "Man oh man."

He hadn't brought his bike that day, so it took him a good fifteen minutes to make his unsteady way back to the house he shared with four other guys. Fortunately, nobody was around when he got there, so he could just fall into bed and let the pain wash over him.

It was dark when he woke much later with a start, the taste of the past twenty-four hours sharp and metallic in his mouth. Music was blasting from the room just outside his door. He groaned and lifted himself gingerly to a sitting position. There was only a trace of the pain left in his head. His muscles were sore, but that was probably just from sleeping so long. Chris belched, loudly, thinking as he did how if his old man were there he would have said, "Nice one, son." He could've laughed, honest to God, the things that made him think of his dad. Belching, for crying out loud. "Nice one, son." Jesus.

It was after nine. Next to the clock on the floor by his bed was a novel he'd started a couple of months ago and hadn't read much more than fifty pages of, most of them more than once because he never made much progress and had to keep going back over what he'd already read to remind himself what had happened. The thought occurred to him that maybe he'd stay in tonight instead of going over to Kelly and what's-her-name's, maybe go get himself a pizza and just stay home and read.

He thought of that boy on the beach, the

mermaid's brother, how he always had a book, was always reading. There was nothing *wrong* with that. Hell, it was good, wasn't it? Better than being an ignoramus like him. He. Him. God, he hated that grammar bullshit. What did it matter? But he guessed maybe it did matter. Maybe Jenny was right. Maybe he was smarter than he let on. If he'd only tried harder. Studied. He still could, right? He could read, go to college. Stuff like that.

"Hey, look who's up!"

The overhead light came on, blinding Chris, who covered his eyes with one hand and threw a pillow with the other.

"Wide by a mile, ya drunken shit-fer-brains!"

He recognized the voice as Todd's, the only one of his housemates he couldn't stomach. Hot Toddy, they called him, the Party Man.

"Yo, Chris, you goin' to Kelly's or what?"

"Maybe," Chris mumbled. "Turn off the light, willya, moron?"

"Yeah, yeah, keep your shirt on, asshole. I just need somethin'. Where's yer wallet?"

Chris was able to open one eye now, barely. Todd, who hadn't turned the light off, was prowling around the room. He was wearing flip-flops, shorts, and what appeared to be a clean T-shirt. For Todd, this was dressed up. As far as Chris was concerned, Todd was a complete slob, even if he *was* wearing a clean T-shirt. But he knew Todd couldn't have cared less what *he* thought. Todd was a couple of years older and he held this quirk of fate over Chris as if the two of them had run a race and Chris had been the loser.

Craig stuck his head in the door. "Hey, buddy, how ya feelin' there? You okay?"

Chris nodded groggily. "I guess I needed the sleep."

"Best medicine."

"I thought that was laughter."

"What?"

"Laughter. You know, the best medicine."

"Oh," Craig said, "yeah, I guess, that, too. So you goin' over to Kelly's or what?"

"I don't know," Chris said. "I thought I'd

maybe, you know, just stay here tonight and—"

"Whoa, what's this?"

Chris looked over to where Todd was standing by his dresser, pulling something out of his wallet.

"Hey," Chris said, "just take ten, all right?"

"No problem," said Todd, pocketing what looked like a twenty. "But what have we here?"

Between his thumb and index finger, he held out a square of folded, yellowing paper. Chris looked on in horror.

"Put that back," he said, his voice full of warning.

"Ooo, methinks it's a love letter," Todd said, shaking the paper open.

Chris lunged and Todd, anticipating the move, jumped out of his way and began reading in a booming voice:

" 'My dear boy.' "

Craig, who had made a move to come to Chris's aid, stopped in his tracks. " 'Dear boy,' " he said, wagging his eyebrows at Chris. "What is this, a letter from your seventh-grade English teacher? What's the story? Did she have the hots for your young bod?"

"Shut up, Craig!" Chris snapped. "I mean it, Todd, I'm not shittin' around here, give me that letter or—"

Todd went on, rapidly, loudly, tauntingly, " 'I love you, dear boy. Even after all these years. I'm sorry I never said the words, but I hope you know they were there inside me. I tried in every way I could to show you. If only you were here now I would tell you every day, every minute, I swear I would, oh my boy . . .' "

Craig, who had been playing an invisible violin, stopped as he watched Chris slump down in the corner of the room and bury his head in his hands. He tried to signal to Todd to stop, but Todd went on dramatically, oblivious to the meaning of the words spewing from his mouth.

" 'My boy, my son. How could I have let you go? I will never forgive myself, never, and I swear I will never love anybody like I loved you. I know you are with the angels and I am here on Earth, but—' "

Todd stopped. He stared at the paper, his mouth hanging open.

"Shit," he said softly.

Craig said, "Give it back to him, Todd. Come on, give it back to him. Let's go."

"But what *is* it?" Todd said, bewildered.

"What difference does it make?" Craig asked. "Just give it back to him, willya."

Todd started toward the corner where Chris was burrowed, then stopped halfway and dropped the paper on the bed. "No harm done, right, buddy?" he said. "I was just playin' around, right? No harm done, no harm done. Okay? We'll catch you later, okay?"

Chris, folded in on himself, didn't move. He could sense Craig walking across the room, coming to a halt near him, squatting down. He could hear Craig's voice: "You okay, bud?" But it was as if he were somewhere else, somewhere deep inside himself that nobody could reach.

"Okay, listen," Craig said, "we'll catch you later. Don't let Todd get to you, man, he's a dick-head, you know that."

A minute later, Chris sensed Craig get up and cross the room.

"Let's go," he heard him say.

And then Todd's voice: "No harm done, right, buddy? You be cool now, Chris. Right? Be cool."

The front door slammed shut, and time passed. He had no idea how much or how little. Just time, that's all, a long stretch of it that held no interest for him. And then—he never even heard her come in—Jenny was there, sitting on the bed. Waiting. Apparently. Waiting for him to say something.

"Just in the neighborhood?"

"I saw Craig. He told me what happened. He said he didn't understand what it was all about, but—"

"The thing is, I had this brother," Chris said, cutting her off. "Sort of. He died before I was born. Drowned in a swimming pool. My dad was working up on a roof, never heard the splash. Got there too late."

"God," Jenny said. "I'm so sorry, Chris."

"It's okay." Funny. How quiet they were talking. How their voices filled the room. "I mean, I never knew him. Him dying before I was born and all. That's why I'm such a good swimmer, though. My folks had me taking lessons from the time I could crawl practically."

Jenny said, "It must have been terrible for them."

"They hardly ever talked about it. For a long time, I thought it was a story I'd made up. Whenever I think about it, it still sounds like a story in my head. 'Once upon a time there was this carpenter and he had a son.' You know, like that."

He looked up. Jenny nodded.

"The first time I figured out that it was something that had really happened was when I heard my old man say—he was sitting out on the front steps of our house talking to this old high school buddy of his, and he said—'I should've been there for him, Tommy. I was supposed to watch out for him. I was his guardian angel.' What a load of shit."

"Chris!"

"Well, it is. There's no such thing as angels. And even if there were, they're not here on Earth. I mean, we're just human, right? We can't make miracles."

"But he was responsible. He's probably felt guilty his whole life."

Chris thought of the paper lying next to Jenny's leg. He thought of the last words, the words Hot Toddy hadn't read aloud. *I know you are with the angels and I am here on Earth, but we are both dead, dear boy. My Michael. Please*

Chris was sure he knew the words his father had intended to write next. *Forgive me.* Had he been unable to face seeing them, or had he passed out before he could write them?

Chris had carried that letter in his wallet since he was in the sixth grade, the time he'd come across his father, drunk, at the kitchen table, writing in the middle of the night to a son who had drowned thirteen years before. He no longer remembered what he had felt when he had looked over his father's unconscious body and first read the words *my dear boy*. Nor did he remember what impulse had made him slip the letter into his bathrobe pocket. He did wonder from time to time what his father had made of the fact that the letter was missing when he'd awoken the next morning. Did he even remember writing it? Did he imagine the angels had hand-delivered it to little Michael in heaven? Little Michael, forever four, not quite five, forever the favorite son?

"What difference does it make?" he said, his eyes level with Jenny's knees. "It doesn't make any difference. The poor kid died, that's the hard, cold truth of it. So I never had a brother. Not really. And all I have of a father is what was left over.

"Hey, shit happens. Isn't that what the T-shirts say? What's the point of talking about it?"

Jenny sighed, out of answers. "What're you going to do now?" she asked. "Do you want me to stay?"

Chris shook his head. "I'd rather be alone," he told her. "Nothing personal."

"Sure," Jenny said. "I understand. I just, I bumped into Craig before. And, you know, he told me . . . I got worried. As long as you'll be okay."

Chris nodded. "I'll be okay," he told her.

"Well, okay, then," Jenny said.

After she was gone, Chris stood up and met his reflection in the mirror over the dresser. The look he saw was the same one he'd seen in the girl's eyes as he was leaving the beach that day. Somebody was in there, screaming to get out, and this time Chris knew for a fact that he wasn't dreaming.

Later, after he'd had a couple of beers to steady his nerves, he headed out the door for Kelly's house in Kismet. The animal was waiting. He could hear it calling his name.

●

"Miranda!" Evario called out. "Where are you going?"

Miranda stopped and waited for her brother the prince to catch up with her.

"I've told you," she said when he slowed beside her, "I cannot sleep in the royal palace. They will worry about me."

Exasperation showed on Evario's face. "They, they," he said impatiently. "You always talk about 'they,' but you will not tell us who they are."

"I'm sorry, Evario," Miranda said. "I wish I could tell you, but it is

it is forbidden

"I'm sorry, Evario," Miranda said. "I know it seems unfair, but years ago I made a promise to the family who took me in when I was washed ashore. I promised that I would stay with them always. They are but poor peasants, and it would break their hearts if I were to leave them."

"But you are with us now," Evario pleaded. "We are your family."

Miranda nodded silently. How could she ever tell Evario the truth?

"Do not despair, good brother," Miranda said at last. "I will find a way to tell them. In time I will be able to leave them."

After Evario turned back, Miranda sat down and began to weep. Her plight felt hopeless. How would she ever be free of the beast?

And then she heard a voice ask, "Child, are you okay?"

Miranda looked up. The angel was standing above her.

"Do not fear me," the angel said. "I will not hurt you. On the contrary, if you believe in me I will help you. Do you believe in me?"

"Oh, yes," Miranda said. "But I am still afraid."

The angel knelt beside the girl and took her

hand. Miranda gasped, fearing the angel's touch. But there was no fire, no pain. To her amazement, the angel's hand was as cool as the waters of the sea.

"You may not always be able to see me," the angel told Miranda. "But I will always be beside you. When you need me, I will be there."

a common shell,
and broken

Evan's mother was crying—softly, but enough to make Evan itchy.

"I shouldn't have said that," he told her. "I'm sorry."

But she just shook her head and said, "Oh, Evan."

For the past hour, they had been walking along the beach, collecting shells in one of Callie's plastic buckets. Callie was spending the day with Sarah's family. Evan's father, looking haunted, had taken the first ferry home that morning. "Unexpected business," he'd told them. A lie so transparent Evan had accepted and forgiven it without question.

"Walk with me," his mother had said to Evan when it was only the two of them left in the house. He had been so relieved she hadn't pushed him to go find friends that he'd quickly consented.

As they walked, Evan checked his mother out of the corner of his eye, at first to see how she was doing, then just to look at her because he liked looking at her. He had always liked looking at her. In the summer, his mother's face was covered with freckles brought out by the sun. When he was five, he had held her face in his small hands and called it a freckle garden. Her sudden laughter had so startled him he'd burst into tears. Seeing that she'd made him cry, she had started crying, too. And then, finding the whole situation hysterically funny, they'd laughed together until they were crying again from laughing so hard. This was Evan's fondest memory of his mother, the one that always came to his mind when he looked at her face in the summertime. It made him love her with a love that ached.

This day, this bright August day as he walked along the beach with his mother, thinking of her freckle-garden face and feeling the familiar ache of love for her, Evan felt a simultaneous pang of hatred for his father. It was not a hatred that was likely to last, but it was real nonetheless, and it went deep, and the reason for it was this: his father had stopped loving his mother as Evan did, with a love that ached.

At least, that's what Evan believed, and that was what was going on inside his head when he said the words that made her cry.

"I'm *never* going to get married," he had announced out of the blue. "Marriage is supposed to be forever, and nothing is forever, so why bother?"

His mother had sunk to the ground then as if the air had gone out of her.

"What's the matter?" Evan said, dropping to his haunches next to her. "Was that bad? What I said, was it bad?"

His mother didn't answer for a long time, other than with her tears, and the shaking of her head, and saying, "Oh, Evan."

They were near the water's edge. A seagull, napping on one leg with its head tucked under its wing, was their only company. It was a gray day, with a cool wind that had kept most people away from the beach and had prompted Evan's mother to put a cotton shawl around her shoulders before they left the house. The shawl was from the gift shop of the Metropolitan Museum of Art in New York City. Evan's father had let him buy it as a birthday gift for his mother, even though it cost far more money than either child had ever been allowed to spend on their parents. She had put it on at once and still wore it often; Evan knew it was one of her favorite things. Now she pulled it tightly around her as if a stronger wind was blowing than actually was.

She reached her hand into the bucket that sat tilted in the sand between them, took out a shell, and held it up for Evan to see. "I've been collecting these this summer," she told him. "Know why?"

Evan shook his head.

"Remember last year? How I wanted only perfect sand dollars? Do you?"

Evan nodded. He thought of all the sand dollars in the basket in his parents' bathroom at home, the hours he and Callie had spent searching for them for their mother, the pride and excitement they had felt when they'd been able to present her with a large one in good condition. Suddenly, Evan recalled how each summer on the first day of their vacation his mother had given them what she called a quest—last year, sand dollars, the year before that periwinkles, the year before that mermaid's purses. But this year, she had given them no instructions; there had been no quest. And what she held in the palm of her hand now was nothing but a common snail shell, and broken at that.

"What do you want that one for?" Evan asked. "It's not perfect."

"That's it," said his mother. "That's just why I want it—*because* it's not perfect. Because it's broken, but still beautiful. Don't you think?"

"Not really," Evan said.

His mother smiled. "When you're young, you don't want anything that isn't perfect.

You think there's something wrong with it."

"The way Callie won't eat any food that's got a spot of brown on it," Evan said.

"You were the same," said his mother.

"No way."

"Of course you were. We all were. We all start out thinking that there *is* such a thing as perfection and that there's something wrong with us if we settle for less. First we won't eat the food with the brown spots. Then we hate ourselves because we have our own brown spots— pimples or ears that are too big or legs that are too skinny."

His mother seemed to be talking more to herself than to him. Evan was getting itchier by the minute.

"And when we imagine the future, the pictures we see in our heads come from magazines or movies. Pretty rooms and a perfect family and a kind of happiness that shines like one of those floors that's just been waxed with the happy housewife standing there admiring her reflection in it. And even when we're grown up, we can't quite shake the idea that perfection is something we're, I don't know, entitled to, somehow."

Evan's mother fell silent. The seagull lifted its head and looked at the two people crouched near it. It blinked at them and yawned, revealing a beak full of feathers.

Evan laughed. "Stupid bird," he said. "Doesn't even know he's got feathers in his mouth."

"Doesn't care," said Evan's mother, laughing, too. "There's a difference."

She turned the shell over in her hand. "Anyway," she said, "the point is this: your dad and I have been going through a hard time lately. I'm sorry I can't tell you what it's about."

"That's not exactly fair," Evan objected.

"It just is what is, Evan. Fair or not. It's something between us. Grown-up stuff. I'm sorry, but that's the way it is. Anyway, there was a point, what was the point? Oh. The shell. The point is that something I thought was perfect has been broken, and I'm having to find the beauty in what is there instead of what I *thought* was there. Like this shell. I can either spend all my time wishing it were perfect, trying to imagine it the way it was or might have been, or I can see how beautiful it is just like this. And it *is* beautiful. To me, at least. To my eyes."

"I don't get it," Evan said.

"No. I guess it probably doesn't make sense if you're thirteen. All I really need you to understand is that Daddy and I still love each other and we are *not* getting a divorce, all right?"

"Who said anything about a divorce? And I'm fourteen, remember?"

"I just don't want you to feel that nothing is forever," Evan's mother went on, "or that you shouldn't get married. Not because of us. We're going to be okay, do you hear me?"

Evan picked up a small, flat stone and tried skipping it against the waves, which he knew, even as he let the stone go, was a pretty pointless thing to do. "Will you tell Callie?" he asked. "She's worried. She has bad dreams every night. She comes to my room."

"Why doesn't she come to me?" Evan's mother asked.

Evan didn't give her an answer because he had none to give.

When they started their walk back home, Evan took his mother's hand. He noticed for the first time how small it was compared to his, and this observation both pleased him and made him unaccountably sad.

Ahead of them, sitting on the top step of the stairway leading from the beach, was the watcher, her body facing their direction.

"That girl is so lonely," Evan's mother said. "I wonder about her, don't you?"

Evan shrugged. "Not really."

"Oh." He could hear the disappointment in her voice. "How can you not wonder about someone who spends every day at the beach where there are so many people and yet keeps herself tucked into her own little world? What does she *think* about all the time?"

"She thinks she's better than everybody else, that's what she thinks," said Evan.

"No," his mother said, giving his hand a hard squeeze. "I can't tell you what she *does* think about, but I *can* tell you that she does *not* think she's better than everybody else. All you have to do is look at her, sweetheart. Look, look at her, what do you see?"

"I don't know," Evan said. "Just some girl. What do you see?"

"A broken shell," said his mother.

As they drew closer, the girl dropped her head, her hair falling over her face like a curtain.

Emboldened by the angel's promise always to be with her, Miranda devised a plan. She would steal the king's crown and offer it to the beast in exchange for her freedom. Although she did not like the thought of stealing from her own father, her real father, she felt certain he would understand once she could tell him the truth, once she was free.

The beast was greedy. Surely he would be appeased by glittering gold and gems of many colors.

Little did Miranda know that even as she devised her plan, the prince and the queen were devising one of their own.

Walking along the water's edge, the queen instructed her son.

"You must follow her, Evario. Poor Miranda hides a secret from us, and we must know what it is."

"But, Mother," said the prince, "what if she is in danger?"

"Do not worry," the queen said, "for the angel watches over her. As for you, my boy . . ."

Here the queen slipped off the wrap she wore about her shoulders.

"This magic cloth will be your shield. Wear it, and no harm shall ever come to you."

and margaret

Amidst.

The word grabbed her attention, as words will do to those who love them, and held her in its power. It wasn't the word alone, but the fact that she had *thought* it, had actually *used* it in a sentence in her own private thoughts, that so fascinated her she sat unable to move.

Here I am amidst their possessions.

It was so literary, so antiquated, that word. How in the world had it found a place in her head?

Silly girl, she said to herself, *your head is the perfect place for words nobody else uses.*

Your head, she thought, *is an orphanage for words.*

A phone rang not three feet from where she was sitting, making her jump up and look back at the hollow left by her body on the edge of the bed.

Goldilocks and the three bears, she thought as the phone continued to ring and she stood there, frozen, waiting for someone to materialize out of thin air to answer it and discover, at the same time, that there was an intruder in the house.

She was the intruder.

What am I doing here?

The phone finally stopped ringing.

She looked around her. She was standing in a strange bedroom in a strange house *amidst their possessions.*

She had never done anything like this in her life.

I'm not doing anything so terrible, she told herself. *I'm just looking.*

Just looking, thank you, she imagined herself saying if someone should come in and find her. *Just looking, thank you.* As if she were in a store, browsing.

But she wasn't in a store, she was in someone's home.

She had never done anything like this.

What am I doing here? she asked herself.

The houses on the island were rarely locked. People went to the beach; the houses stood empty, open. It was surprising, people often said, how few burglaries there were. Oh, there was the occasional petty theft, it was true, a few dollars left lying on a kitchen counter. But nothing more. Almost never.

I didn't come here to take anything, she told herself. *I'm just looking. I just want to see . . .*

She picked up the shawl she had observed the mother wearing on the beach the day before. It was lying across the foot of the bed, inches from the impression made by her own bottom.

Bottom, foot, inches, she thought.

She held the shawl up before her. *Just looking.*

She brought it to her face, inhaled its fragrance of wind and sea salt and mother.

She wrapped it around her shoulders as she walked slowly about the room, looking, touching.

Reading glasses.

Nasal spray.

Hairbrush.

She pulled a few hairs away from the bristles of the brush, studied them in the palm of her hand. They were reddish brown. The mother's hair.

Auburn tresses.

Seersucker robe thrown across a chair.

Seersucker.

Pile of books on the floor by the bed. She bent to pick each one up in turn, careful to memorize the exact angle of its relationship to the one beneath, so that no one would suspect the books had been disturbed. That Goldilocks had been there.

The phone rang again.

"Oh!" she exclaimed like a character in a play. Whose need was so urgent they called twice within five minutes? Twice within five minutes was a lot for a beach house on an August afternoon. It was important, must be an emergency.

She had the crazy notion that it was her mother calling, asking her what she was doing there. Or her father, demanding to know why she never went to the beach with them, where she went off to on her own every day, if he'd known *this* was what she was up to, prowling around in other people's houses . . . *Well, young lady, we'll just see about that.*

But I've never done this before. I don't know what made me do it, I just had to see. I was curious. There was this family on the beach, and I just had to see.

See what, young lady, if you don't mind my asking, you just had to see what?

She picked up the receiver.

"Karen?"

It was a man's voice on the other end.

"Karen? Hello? Callie, Evan?"

It was not her father's voice. A man's voice, but not her father's. Of course it wasn't her father's. How would he have known she was there?

Quickly, she hung up the phone.

What have I done? she thought. *They'll know someone was in the house.*

She had to get out. Quickly, before she was discovered.

But what about the upstairs? She had to see the children's rooms, the boy's, the sister's. Their rooms were upstairs. She had to see them. But what would she do if someone came in? If someone found her, what would she say?

I had to use the bathroom. I'm sorry, I know I shouldn't be here, but I was sick. I had to get to a bathroom before . . .

Yes.

And if she had to: *The phone rang. I wasn't thinking. I picked it up. I sort of freaked out, I didn't say anything. I'm sorry. Please don't tell my parents I was here. I didn't hurt anything. I didn't take anything. I just had to use the bathroom. I was sick. And then the phone rang.*

She was standing in Callie's room now (she didn't remember climbing the stairs), holding a photograph in her hand. She didn't sit on the bed. She didn't want to leave an indentation.

Had she thought to brush away the indentation on the parents' bed in the room downstairs?

There were so many things to think of. She had never done this before.

And what had possessed her to pick up the phone?

But it didn't matter. None of it mattered. The photograph was all that mattered. It was why she was here. She hadn't known before why she had come, but now . . .

This is my family. I took the picture, that's why I'm not in it. We were at the beach. We love the beach. We go every summer, rent a house for a whole month. That's my dad. He's an artist. He's famous, you might have heard of him. I mean, if you know about artists. My mother is beautiful, isn't she? She used to be a dancer. Ballet. But when she had children, us, when she had us, she stopped. She says she doesn't regret it, not one bit. She loves being a mother. She says it's the best job in the whole world, and she feels sorry for men because it's one thing they can't do and it's the best job there is.

That's my brother Evan. He's really neat. We've always gotten along, even when we were little. He taught me how to swim. And we go snorkeling together. *Do you know how to snorkel? Evan and I do. Our parents have taken us on vacations to the Caribbean just so Evan and I can go snorkeling. We have seen the most beautiful fish. Colors you can't imagine. Evan and I have swum with dolphins.*

And that's Callie. Isn't she cute? She loves it when Evan and I make her into a sand mermaid. The summer this picture was taken, I taught her how to fly a kite. Callie and I like to bake together. Every year on Valentine's Day we bake a cake for our parents. It's in the shape of a heart, and we decorate it with fancy icing. Pink and white roses. And the words "We love you." Callie and Evan and I, we—

The phone rang a third time. She raced down the stairs and out of the house. As she crossed the porch, she grabbed up the kite she'd once seen the boy and his sister flying. Only later did she think what a foolish thing it had been to take it. Lucky for her no one had seen her carrying it. Now it would have to remain hidden in the crawl space under her house. Forever.

In her bedroom, she folded the mother's

shawl neatly and tucked it, together with the framed photograph, between the mattress and box spring of her bed.

That night, after she was fairly certain her parents were asleep, she removed the photograph from its frame. On the back was written:

Saltaire. Karen, Jeffrey, Evan, Callie.

It was dated August of the previous year.

She set to work immediately. Everything she needed was right there, under her bedcovers where she'd hidden them: the flashlight she had sneaked from the drawer in the kitchen, scissors, tape. And the snapshot of herself she'd taken from her mother's purse when her mother had been out for a walk late that afternoon. It would have been nicer if she were smiling in the picture, but she couldn't remember the last time she'd smiled for a camera. Even her school photos were pretty grim. At least this wasn't a school photo. A school photo would never have done. Luckily, she was wearing a T-shirt in the snapshot. A bathing suit would have been better, but a T-shirt would do just fine.

Carefully, silently (she had thought to put a drop of oil on the scissors earlier so they wouldn't make a sound), she began to cut away the background until she held herself in her hand. Just herself.

Just me, all alone, nothing around me, not even air.

She put the cutout of herself down and picked up the other photograph, inserting the sharpest tip of the scissors—one end came to a finer point than the other—into a spot directly behind Evan's left shoulder. Up over his shoulder the scissors went, up around the curve of his neck . . .

Up, up. Easy, don't cut into his head. That's it. Around his head, get the ear, don't cut off the ear. Vincent van Gogh, she thought. *Down the neck, around the shoulder, down the arm, to Callie now, across her shoulder, careful, easy now, to the middle of her head, stop.*

She knew exactly how much to cut and where. She picked up the cutout of herself and slid it into the slot she'd made in the family photograph. It fit perfectly. So, she thought, did she.

One piece of tape across the back, one rolled-up piece of tape behind her head, and now, if she held the picture at arm's length and squinted her eyes just a little . . .

Not a lot, just a little . . .

She looked like she actually belonged. Like she had always been a part of the photograph.

This is my family. That's me and my brother Evan and my sister Callie. Everybody says Callie and I look alike, but I think they say that because we both look so much like our mother. Don't you think? Don't you think we look like our mother?

Before putting the picture back in its frame (where the glass would flatten her handiwork even more, creating an almost perfect illusion), before sliding it back under the mattress along with the flashlight and scissors and tape, the neatly folded shawl, she had one last thing to do.

and Margaret, she wrote on the back of the picture, so that it read:

Saltaire. Karen, Jeffrey, Evan, Callie and Margaret.

●

What joy Miranda felt! Her plan worked! The beast accepted the king's crown in exchange for her freedom!

"Now we shall be together always," the girl told her family after they had listened to her tale.

"My poor daughter," the queen said, wiping away the tears that stained her face. "To think that you were held prisoner all these years by a cruel beast. Why did you not let us help you escape?"

"The beast is too powerful," the girl said. "I was afraid he would hurt you."

"I tried to follow you one night," said Evario, "but you were too fleet of foot. I could not keep up."

"No matter now," Miranda said, beaming. "For we are together at last. And nothing shall

Oh God the beast. The beast. I hate the beast!! He killed my

Miranda's family. He came in the night and slaughtered them all!

And took Miranda prisoner again! And told her if she ever tried to escape again he would kill her, too! He would tear her limb from limb, just as he had torn her family apart! There is no power greater than the beast's!!

angel
where are you

the center cannot hold

It was all coming apart.

That's what Evan felt.

The whole world was going crazy, or maybe it was just his little piece of the world, he couldn't say. All he knew was that everything felt different, upside down.

There was this line from a poem he'd read in eighth grade that went: "Things fall apart; the center cannot hold." Once he'd heard those words he'd never been able to get them out of his head, and he knew why. The weekend after his class had studied that poem he and Callie had been sent to stay with their aunt and uncle in Connecticut. When they returned home late Sunday afternoon, their parents were changed, different. It was the beginning of the closed doors and long silences.

Things fall apart.

It was eleven o'clock. He had come down to the beach by himself because Callie was still sleeping and their mother didn't want her to be in the house alone. Callie had hardly slept the night before. She couldn't sleep, she said, without the photograph. Their mother, holding Callie in her lap and stroking her hair, had said to her it was only a snapshot, they probably had the negative at home; assured her she still had a family, there would be no divorce. And Callie had said through her tears, "I almost believe you."

But in the middle of the night, Callie had come to Evan. "I had a bad dream. It was the house where the sad music was playing. Remember from last week? When you and me and Sarah went biking?"

"Yeah."

"Well, I was inside that house. I mean, not really, because I don't know what it's like in there since I've never been in there for real, but you know how in your dreams everything makes sense." Evan acknowledged that he did.

"So I was inside the house and it was dark and this sad music was playing, like somebody had died, and I was the only one there and I kept going through all these doors and I couldn't find anybody. And I was getting more and more scared all the time. And then there was one last door. And the singing—remember how it was a woman singing that time we heard it?—well, the singing was coming from behind that door. I went to open it, and just when I did it changed to crying. Then I woke up."

When Evan had finally fallen back to sleep somewhere after four, he could tell from Callie's breathing that she was still awake. He remembered hearing her say (or perhaps he dreamed it), "Evan, do you know what I wish?" But he had no memory of her answer. She must have gone back to her own bed at some point because when he woke up in the morning, he was alone.

"My shawl is missing, too," his mother said in place of *good morning* when he found her on the porch, coffee mug in hand, rocking.

"Did you move the kite?" he asked her. The day before, he had left it leaning against the rocker.

"No," she said. And then: "I think I'd better call the police."

Evan was sure he knew who the thief was. "I'll take care of it," he told his mother. *I won't be one of these very yellow guys.* And for some reason, she agreed to let him.

Evan had expected to find Shane on the beach, but was glad when he wasn't there. It gave him time to think about what he would say.

Give them back, Shane. You had your fun, your "entertainment value." Now give them back! Or I'll . . . I'll break your face. I'll hurt you, Shane, I swear it. I don't care if you're stronger than me or if you've got your stupid gang. I won't let you hurt my sister or my mother. You can't take their things. I don't care about the kite, keep the stupid kite, but give back the other stuff. Come on, do it! Do it now, Shane, or . . .

Evan looked over at the lifeguard stand for the tenth time that morning. Chris still wasn't there. Evan needed him to be.

Hey, Chris, teach me how to be a hero.

But Chris was missing in action. So, Evan noticed, was the watcher.

Where was everybody?

Was everybody sick?

Hey, Chris!

Hey, watcher-girl!

Hey, Dad!

His father was missing, too, had gone home, wouldn't say when he was coming back even though there was only a week left of vacation. Evan's mother kept saying everything would be fine, they loved each other, it was grown-up stuff, sorry she couldn't tell them what was going on, there would be no divorce, everything would be fine.

"I almost believe you," Callie had said.

Shane had stolen their things, had come right into their house and stolen their things, had even picked up the phone when his father called.

Crazy.

Hey, Shane . . .

What would he *really* say to Shane?

The thought of it made him feel sick. He pictured Shane surrounded by his gang. The boys in black. It looked in his mind like a scene from a movie. Problem was, Evan was no kickboxer, no karate-chopper, no quick-draw good guy who could wipe out the bad guys singlehanded.

He would go to Shane's house. Maybe he'd get lucky and Shane would be alone. It would be easier if it was just the two of them. Shane probably had the stuff at his house, anyway. He would just turn it over.

"No big deal," he'd say. "It was just for fun, man. Lighten up."

Evan checked out the lifeguard stand. Jenny was sitting up there next to some guy who wasn't Chris. Evan needed to talk to Chris. Chris would know what to do.

Suddenly he was at the base of the stand, not exactly looking up at the guards but not exactly *not* looking up. "Excuse me," he said.

"Sorry?" It was Jenny's voice. "Did you say something?"

Evan raised his head. "I was wondering, do you know where the other lifeguard is, you know, the one you usually work with?"

"Chris?"

"I guess." Evan hated when he said *I guess* when he knew perfectly well what he was talking about. It was like the time he'd asked Shane what his name was when he already knew.

"Chris is gone," Jenny said.

"Where is he?" Evan asked, not letting himself make sense of what Jenny was telling him.

Jenny said, "He's gone. Home."

"Home?" Evan repeated.

"You need something?" the other guard asked.

"No."

"Did you need to talk to Chris?" Jenny asked.

"No. I mean, I sort of did, but it's okay. That's okay."

Evan started to walk away when Jenny's voice stopped him.

"He might still be here," she called out.

"I think he said he was going to take the one o'clock ferry. If it's important . . ."

Evan turned to her. His face must have given her the answer because she went on without waiting for him to speak. "His house is on Neptune," she told him, "the second one in from the bay."

one real thing, not magic

"Ma, fer cryin' out loud, will you stop it? I told ya already, they don't need me here anymore. . . . What? . . . I told ya. The season's winding down. . . . No, I'm not a quitter. Since when am I a quitter?"

Chris sat on the edge of his stripped bed, bouncing his legs up and down on the balls of his feet and wondering what the hell had possessed him to call home. He supposed he had to; he had no place else to go and he figured it was better to give them some warning than just to show up. Now he wasn't so sure.

"Listen, don't start that college bullshit with me again, will ya? . . . What? . . . Oh, so now yer gonna get on my case 'cause I say 'bullshit,' gimme a break. . . . Huh? . . . I don't know. . . . That's what I said. I don't know if

I'm going to California. I need some time. . . .
No, I'm not going to just hang around. Geez,
don't you think I want a life, too? . . . No way
will I work with Dad. . . . Hey, listen, he doesn't
want me to work with him any more than
I want to. You know what he said to me when
I . . . wait, wait, don't interrupt, I'm telling
you something . . . you know what he said to
me when I tried to help him with that Delaney
job? He told me I had clumsy hands. Nice,
huh? Did I deserve that? . . . Oh, don't start
defending him now, okay? Spare me, all right?"

A timer went off in the kitchen.

"I gotta go," Chris said into the phone. "I'll
see you at dinnertime. . . . No, I'm not running
away from our conversation. Where do you
get that crap? You're watching too many of
those talk shows. . . . I gotta take my lunch out
of the oven, okay? . . . Yes, I can cook. I can
take care of myself. . . . Yeah, fine, it's frozen,
what do you care? Listen, I gotta go. . . . Yeah,
fine, I love you, too. I'll be home around six. . . .
What? . . . Yeah, of course, you can tell Dad,

why wouldn't ya? He won't care anyway, he doesn't give a shit. . . . Yeah, I gotta go, too. . . . All right. . . . I'll see ya later, all right."

Chris hung up the phone and counted slowly to ten. If he didn't, he would probably have had to yell or throw something and break it. By the time he got to the kitchen, his chicken pot pie had bubbled over and made a mess on the bottom of the oven.

"That's their problem," he muttered with satisfaction as he turned off the timer.

Giving the steaming pie time to cool off, Chris popped open a can of beer. *Why am I going home?* he thought. It wasn't even his home anymore. He didn't want it to be. Problem was, he had no idea what he did want.

Except. And this was crazy, he knew that, but the one thing he wanted was to save his brother. He wanted to travel back in time and be eighteen years old, just like he was now, and be standing there at the edge of the pool when his brother fell in. He wanted to dive into that water and pull his brother out and save his father's life.

And save my father's life, Chris thought.

Chris thought, *If my brother had lived, he would be older than me. Who knows, maybe he would have been married by now, have a kid. I'd be an uncle. My dad would be a grandpa.*

Funny, Chris thought, *I always think of him as younger than me, my kid brother. That's because he'll always be four. But the truth is he would have been older than me. Maybe he would have taught me a few things. Maybe he would have been here now to tell me what to do.*

Even now, Chris wasn't sure why he'd quit his job. He just knew he couldn't do it anymore. He was through lifeguarding. It got to be, in his head, this pressure and this need all rolled up in one to save somebody's life, to prove he could do it. No, the opposite: to prove he wouldn't blow it. The longer it didn't happen, the more the pressure and the need built up inside him and the harder he partied at night and the sicker he felt during the day. The animal was consuming him. He had to get out.

It hadn't taken him long to pack. He could

eat his lunch, have another beer, be down at the dock in plenty of time. He'd already said his goodbyes. Last night, Jenny had told him she was disappointed in him. Chris had told her to shove it, which on reflection may have been an overreaction. Still, she had come around in the morning to apologize. She'd said, what is it she'd said? Oh, right, that she'd only meant she cared about him.

He was a good guy, Jenny had told him. He had a lot more going on inside than most guys she knew. What had she called him? "A hunk with a heart of gold."

A piece of chicken caught in Chris's throat. Damn. Why did Jenny have to say those things? What did she have to care about him for? He'd told her that morning he was going to miss her. It had come out of his mouth like one of those automatic things you say, but then he'd said it again.

"No, honest, Jen. I'm gonna miss you."

It wasn't like he loved her or anything. She was not remotely his type. But all those hours up there on the stand together, they'd developed this special thing between them. At least he'd felt that way. They hadn't even talked all that much, not as much as Jenny would have liked them to, for sure, but he'd gotten to, what? trust her? Yeah. Trust her.

"Shit," Chris said, tossing the rest of the pot pie in the garbage, "now I got nobody to trust."

One time during his senior year the school counselor had asked Chris, "If you could do one thing to change your life—one real thing, not magic—what would it be?" Chris had sat there for what felt like an hour, and the only things he could think of were the magic kind. The counselor, who was this really nice and dynamite-looking lady who happened to have the name of Miss Fox, finally reached over and touched the back of Chris's hand and said, looking him straight in the eye, "That's your question, Chris. Don't let it go until you've answered it."

So was Miss Fox to blame for the mess his head was in this summer?

Hey, it wasn't her fault he couldn't answer a simple question.

Chris glanced at his watch. He had about an hour. Maybe he'd kill some time going for a walk. In all the time he'd been out on the island, he'd never just gone for a walk. Not for its own sake. It wasn't too late. He could go for one now, and, what the hell, if he missed the one o'clock, there was always another ferry at three. And the five-thirty after that. He could always call his mother, tell her he'd be getting in later. Tell her to tell the old man not to wait up.

Thing was, Chris didn't want to go home. Not really. It was just, he didn't have anyplace else to go.

where the sad music
played

Evan was halfway to Chris's house when he changed his mind. He had sort of known all along he *would* change his mind. To be honest, he had known all along he was kidding himself if he thought he would go through with asking Chris for help. Every time he had tried coming up with what he would say, he'd sounded like a naïve little kid. Or worse, like somebody who had a crush on somebody and was trying to suck up to them.

When he reached Neptune, Chris's street, he hesitated only briefly before continuing on to Shane's house.

Hey, Shane, how's it going?

What do you want? What did you say your name was again?

Evan. My name is Evan. We hung out together once, remember? Remember how you tried to get me to steal those sunglasses?

So?

So that's how I know you like to steal things. That's why I'm here.

What are you, a cop or something?

Evan smiled. *I ought to write for TV,* he thought. But then he thought, *What if he denies it? And what if his mother is there? Oh, hi, Mrs. Whatever-your-name-is, I'm here to accuse your son of being a thief.*

He almost turned back. But then he thought of Callie. And his mother. And he decided no matter how it turned out, he had to confront Shane. At the worst, he'd be called a liar. At the best, he'd get their things back and be a hero.

It took him five minutes of standing behind a huge mess of blueberry bushes out front of Shane's house to work up the nerve to do what he'd planned: walk up the ramp, knock on the door, open his mouth, say, *Hey, Shane, we gotta talk.* Except he never got beyond the part where he knocked on the door.

Nobody was home.

Evan waited, then knocked again and waited some more.

At first, he couldn't believe his luck. Then he thought he must have been nuts to imagine Shane would actually be at home anyway.

Like he was just going to wait around for me. Like: Hey, Evan, thanks for dropping by. Here's your stuff. Have a nice day.

Evan walked away, his threats undelivered, the promises he'd made to himself unfulfilled. He was trying to decide what to do next when he became aware of the music. A woman was singing just the way Callie had described it when she told him her dream: as if somebody had died.

When Evan came to the crosswalk, the music made him stop. He could have said he paused to listen, but it wasn't like that. It was more like the music had this long arm that stretched out from the house and wrapped itself around him, holding him while this voice cried in his ear. *Evan, I am so sad, do you hear it? Do you hear how sad I am? Evan, Evan, I am crying. My heart is breaking. I am full of sorrow and pain.*

Evan stood there, unable to move, in a dream. *In Callie's dream,* he thought, *the house was dark and she was all alone, except for the voice behind the door.*

He heard footsteps in the distance. He turned. Someone was walking toward him. It looked like Chris, but it couldn't have been. Chris was going home, was maybe already gone.

The music pulled Evan slowly to the bay end of the street until he stood facing a dark house nearly lost in overgrown shrubs and thick reeds. It sounded like the same opera he had heard coming from the house when he'd passed by another time. After a sobbing crescendo, as if it had accomplished what it had set out to do, the music stopped.

A buoy bell clanged in the bay, a dove cooed, everywhere insects were buzzing. Then the music again began to play.

In a speckle of sunlight, something shiny winked at Evan from under the house. Silver, then turquoise, then bright, bright yellow.

Evan squatted down. There in the crawl space beneath the front deck was his kite. His heart pounding, he moved as quietly as he could under the house until his hands could touch it: the kite his father had bought, the kite that had made Evan feel he was flying.

He remembered: there was someone else the kite had made feel that way.

She was the thief who had come into his house.

This was her house. Where the sad music played.

Evan cautiously made his way back along the ramp, then up it to the window by the front door. It took a moment for his eyes to adjust to the darkness inside. Even then, he couldn't make sense of what he was seeing.

A kitchen.

Two people standing at the sink.

A man. Tall, wearing pants and no shirt. Hair

on his shoulders. Big arms, barrel-chested. Strong.

A girl.

The man holding the girl's head down in a sink full of water.

Evan could see the water.

He thought, *The man is washing the girl's hair.* But the water wasn't running. There was no shampoo he could see. There was no movement. The girl's body was bent awkwardly over the sink, her hands dangling at her sides, her head under the water. The man's outstretched arm remained rigid. Its strength was almost frightening.

Evan thought, *If the man is not washing the girl's hair . . .*

Suddenly, the man's hand turned into a fist, gathering up strands of the girl's hair as if they were stubborn weeds to be pulled from the earth and yanked her head out of the water. The girl gasped and spat out water and made choking sounds and said, "Please, Dad." And the man said, "I don't think you've learned your lesson."

On the table in the center of the room was Callie's photograph, the frame and glass smashed, the picture torn.

Evan looked up as the girl turned toward the window and saw him. Her eyes were like the music, calling to him.

The man's hand plunged the girl's head back under the water. The girl's arms flew wildly about, then clutched the edge of the sink and held on.

Evan ran so fast his legs burned.

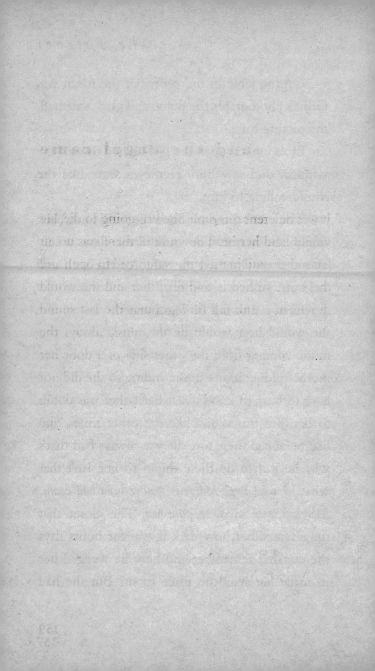

and the angel came

It was different this time. She was going to die. He would hold her head down until there was no air left in her until her mouth was forced to open and the water rushed in and filled her and she would drown in a sink full of water and the last sound she would hear would be the music always the music coming from the other side of a door her mother hiding in her music, hiding so she did not have to hear, to know what her father was doing to her. But this wasn't like the other times. She had been bad then, too, she was always bad that's why he had to do these things to her. Isn't that what he told her? *Margaret, you've been bad again. Margaret, you must be punished.* The closet that time, remember how dark it was for hours days she couldn't remember and how he wedged her in made her stand no place to sit? But she had deserved it. She always deserved it. Even now. Even now. Especially now, hadn't he told her this was the worst thing she'd ever done to him hadn't she sent him into a rage this time didn't she deserve it? Oh God she couldn't breathe but he would not lift her head he would hold it there until . . .

Please Evario boy at the window face at the window please don't leave me. Make him stop make him stop.

Suddenly her head was out of the water, her father's hand gripping her hair, she could stand the pain, the pain didn't matter, what mattered was air and now she was gulping it down, coughing, spitting, she felt like a sponge, her face wet from water wet from tears and spit and the watery snot leaking from her nose. She was nothing but a sponge her father could fill with water and wring out and fill again.

"Please, Dad, stop."

He was her father, he loved her, didn't he tell her all the time he loved her? Didn't he tell her he punished her because he loved her? Because when she was bad . . .

No time to look to the window. She was under again. Was he still there the boy the mermaid-maker the prince the brother her brother? All the times and the bad times the bad things she had done he had never punished her like this even the tub of icy water she'd had to sit in till she was blue and her mother had wrapped her in all those towels and blankets even then she had survived survived the hitting and the pinching and the twisting but she could not survive this. *Oh God why did I let him see the picture the shawl but it was the picture that made him crazy.*

Aren't we good enough for you, Margaret, your mother and I? Is this where you've been going off to every day, off to join your other family? What lies do you tell them about us, Margaret? Do you tell them your father is mean to you when you know he loves you, when you know he only hurts you sometimes because you're a bad child and he loves you and wants to make you good? Look at this, Margaret, look at this picture . . . your mother says you stole this picture right out of her wallet, cut it up, and all for what, to stick your face into some other family where it doesn't belong, as if for godsake child they'd ever want a bad apple like you.

But, Margaret thought, *I never showed him the picture. I never would have. He took it. He came into my room when I wasn't there, searched it, must have searched it because the picture and the shawl were under the mattress, thank God my notebook is nowhere he'll ever find it ever see what I've written. But he came looking, looking for what, looking for anything I might be keeping from him, might be hiding from him. I'm not bad. He's bad. I've known for a long time . . . what? What have I known for a long time? What have I known?*

She felt the yank, didn't know if it was her father's hand pulling her out of the water or the angel of death. The room was a blur. She was crying, whimpering, babbling, not knowing what she was saying. A sideways glance to the window told her the boy was gone.

All hope.

Gone.

She was thinking so many things at once it was as if her thoughts were on different floors and her mind was an elevator out of control racing up and down, the doors flashing open to let the thoughts in but not let her out.

The music, the same, the sad . . .

His hand . . .

Did I imagine the boy at the window . . .

Am I bad, really, am I . . .

My head . . .

If I drown, if I die . . .

The music, the same, the sad, will she play it at my funeral . . .

Will there be a funeral, who will come, what friends do I have . . .

Will anyone ever know the truth, what happened to me . . .

What is the truth? Am I bad . . .

No, I'm not . . .

I'm a good girl, you're a bad girl, Margaret . . .

What are you doing in our house?

I didn't mean anything, I was just looking, I was sick, I had to use the bathroom.

I'm sick.

"Please, Dad, stop."

No warning this time, her head under, she wasn't ready, couldn't breathe, had no choice even if it meant she would be punished later, if there was a later; she put whatever strength she had left into her hands rolled them into fists and struck out blindly somewhere out there was her father she hit him as hard as she could she wasn't thinking about what she was doing she was just trying to survive to survive just trying to survive . . .

And now as her strength began to leave her she floated up to the ceiling yes floating watching the way she always did, watching herself, not herself but her body watching as he did whatever he did to her body, pulling herself away from the pain and the humiliation the hate YES the hate. Somewhere safe. If she could find somewhere safe she could endure it endure anything. Up there on the ceiling looking down watching as she always did, safe, away from Margaret, it was happening to that girl Margaret *but not me, I am here, Margaret is just the name of that body that he is hurting,* but this time it was different. Even as she watched herself try to save herself she knew she was watching herself die because this time he would let her die this time she had gone too far, been too bad. *And the beast will kill me.*

But then she heard (did she? did she hear it?) a voice shouting: "STOP!"

And her head was ripped from the water like a baby near to death is ripped from the womb before it suffocates, before it dies before it can live. She began to retch, her body heaving as water poured out of her mouth, her nose, her eyes. All of her was crying.

Her father's hand was no longer on her. He moved away as another came toward her. She saw (it made no sense but she saw) that it was the angel who approached and not the angel of death. It was her angel and behind him the prince Evario the prince her brother the boy at the window, they had come yes they were there they would not let her die they had heard her prayers . . .

The angel put his arms around her (she

could smell the sea on them), held her until her body was still until she felt herself falling lightly through the air, a single feather floating, drifting . . .

"You'll be okay now," the angel told her, his voice folding around her like clouds like powdery wings.

"Get your hands off my daughter," she heard her father say. "I ought to call the police."

"Why don't you just do that?" the angel replied. "I'm sure the police would be interested to know what's been going on here."

Her father's face was a red wound dissected by the thin white scar of his lips. Or was it fire, his face? *Burn,* she thought, *burst into flame and be nothing but ashes I can sweep away.*

His eyes narrowed as he caught her looking at him. Ashamed, she turned away. The boy stood on the other side of the table, staring down at the ruined photograph of his family. Margaret wanted to tell him she was sorry, that she hadn't meant to steal it, but she couldn't, she didn't have the words. Besides, she was afraid that maybe all of this was a dream, that she had died and was dreaming, that if she spoke she would awaken and be dead.

She noticed her mother then, standing in the open doorway to the next room, the music still playing behind her. Her face was a mirror of Margaret's own: dazed, as if waking from a dream or in the middle of one.

"I'd like to see you prove a damn thing," she heard her father growl. "You barge in here and start accusing me of God knows what—"

"Nobody's accused you of anything, sir," the angel said calmly.

"You're damn straight. And I wouldn't start, if I were you. Because it's your word against mine. And who are they going to believe? I'm the girl's father."

"That doesn't give you any right," the boy said, his voice trembling yet clear and pointed as a shard of glass. "I saw you. I watched through that window and I saw what you were doing. I'll tell the police just like I told Chris. I'm not afraid of you."

Margaret's father took a step in the boy's direction, then stopped. "You know what I think?" he said, his color returning to normal, his thin lips widening into the salesman's smile he flashed first at the boy, then at the angel. Margaret was aware that he never even acknowledged her mother's presence. "I think there's been a misunderstanding. Let me ask you, son: what exactly did you see when you looked in the window?"

"I saw you holding her head underwater," the boy said, indicating Margaret. "Same as when I came back with Chris."

Her father chuckled. "You see? That's what I mean. What we've got here is a misunderstanding. My little girl's afraid of swimming. I ask you, have you seen her in the water once this summer? Hm? Have you? Either of you?"

He waited until both boys slowly shook their heads.

"That's because she's afraid. She said to me . . . she said to me, 'Daddy, I'm afraid of drowning, that's why I won't swim. If you could teach me to breathe underwater, maybe I wouldn't be scared.' That's all I was doing, boys. Ask her if you don't believe me, just ask; she's a good girl, she'll tell you the truth. Aren't you, Margaret, aren't you a good girl?"

She couldn't look at him. If she did, she'd never be able to speak the truth. What if she *did* tell the truth, what if she opened her mouth and let the truth pour out of her pure and undisguised, no more stories, no more angels and beasts and dolls and princes, but the truth the truth . . .

My father hurts me.

It would be so easy. Four words. All she had to do was let one word take the hand of the next and the next and lead them out of her into the open, let everyone hear them. Let everyone hear the truth.

But the truth confused her. It always did. She *was* afraid of swimming. *That* was the truth. *Had* she asked her father to help her learn to breathe underwater? Maybe she'd forgotten. Maybe she *thought* she was being punished, but maybe that wasn't it at all.

"Why don't you boys run along now?" her father said.

The angel's hands loosened their hold on her shoulders. The boy began to back away from the table. She wanted to cry out: *Don't leave me!* But if she did, her punishment would only be that much greater.

"You're good boys," her father continued smoothly. "I'd hate to have to make any trouble for you, so why don't you just—"

A door closed. A lock fell into place, and from behind the locked door her mother shrieked, "No more! No more!" Suddenly the music was growing louder and louder until the force of it nearly shook the house.

Margaret's father raced across the room where he threw himself against the door, pounding it with hammer fists. But it would not budge, and the music blared. "Goddamn you, Helen!" he bellowed. "What are you trying to do to me? Do you want the police here again? Is that what you want?"

The deafening music was his only answer. When at last he turned away his face was pale as ashes, the fire gone. *My mother,* Margaret thought, *has betrayed him.* As if he could read her mind, he looked at her and hissed, "Are you happy now?" Running his beefy tongue over his dry lips: "Are you happy?"

His question ran through her like an electric shock—not merely because of the meanness behind it, his pitiful last stab at wounding her—but because deep down she knew the answer was yes. Yes, even if she couldn't feel it yet, yes, she was happy. She would be. Someday.

The boy asked, "What should we do, Chris?"

"Nothing to do," the angel answered. "Just wait. Wait here with Margaret until we know she's okay."

It didn't take long for the policeman to arrive. He'd been to the house before. This time the music was so loud he hadn't even had to wait for a complaint. He'd heard it himself from six blocks away.

Charging up the ramp, he shouted out, "What the hell is going on in there? Haven't I told you people—"

When he threw open the door, the music stopped abruptly. All that was left were the cicadas and the doves and somewhere in the distance a foghorn calling, and then a key turning in a lock.

When Margaret's mother came into the room tears were streaming down her face as if a dam had burst somewhere inside her.

The policeman looked from one face to the next. "What the hell is going on?" he repeated.

Margaret saw the boy's eyes forgive her. She felt the angel's hands gently squeeze her shoulders, then release her. She took a step, a small step, toward the policeman. As she did, she felt or thought she felt a slight breeze behind her; she heard or thought she heard a rustling of wings. She closed her eyes and imagined them filling the room, those wings, those white powdery wings, powerful and soft and there to hold her whenever she needed them, as she needed them now to hold her, now as she opened her eyes and parted her lips and set free the truth.

"My father," she said, "hurts me."

and the angel came
and the beast was slain
and the doll's enchantment fell away
and the mother the real mother the true mother
who had been locked inside the doll held the girl and
begged her forgiveness and
someday
the girl would give her forgiveness
and then
the mother would sing a song
and it would be
it would be
a happy song
and the girl would be safe at last
and Margaret
yes
I am Margaret
and Margaret would be safe at last